"Anything for You"

By

Amy Braybrook

This Book is dedicated to my Beautiful Daughter Maddison, as I want to show her that anything is possible when you follow your dreams!

———

It is also in honour of all those that we have loved and sadly lost.

All the characters in this book are fictional
characters and not based on any real person

Chapter One

Chloe Hunter was 25 years old and lived in her home town of Peterborough, in a little village on the outskirts of the town, which is where she had lived all her life, and she still lived in the same house she had done since she was born. She could still remember so clearly, the many trips to and from school, stopping off at the little bakery on the way home for an iced finger bun, or two, playing in the park at the weekend, as well as the summer holidays trying to put little shows on in the garden with her best friend Scarlett, they were still quite young at the time, so it needed some work but it was great fun. She could also still remember the family traditions they had at Christmas, Mum would always display the things she had made at school, no matter what they looked like, her dad would always lift her up so she could put the star on top of the tree and Mum would tweak the baubles for days, as she liked everything to be just right and Chloe would try sneaking the chocolates from the back of tree so no one would notice but she always got caught. She had so many lovely memories, but there were some extremely sad memories too, which she tried to forget, as she didn't want to remember those things.

Chloe was such a beautiful young lady, with bright piercing blue eyes, and blonde hair in tight curls down to her shoulders, she was petite and she dressed in a feminine, girl next door type of way, she was the sort of girl that everyone wanted to be like, as she was so kind and caring to everyone that she met, but she was also the type of girl that boys wanted to be with as she was just so pretty and had her head screwed on, she wasn't stupid, far from it, she was very intelligent, she had her mother's brains and beauty.

On the surface everyone thought that Chloe was confident, happy and content but beneath all the things people thought they saw, not many actually knew the truth of just what she had been through in her life so far. Chloe had not had a typical childhood, not like most children anyway as she had grown up with a life riddled with pain, heartbreak and confusion, and most of the time she didn't feel any of the things that people thought she was.

Life had never been the same for Chloe since the tragic day, one Friday afternoon, when she came home and found her mum Elizabeth lying on their sofa not moving or breathing, her dad had picked her up from school, and while he was sorting her things out in the hallway, Chloe had walked in to the living room first and found her mum there, and at first she just thought her mum was sleeping, but she was actually dead, she had committed suicide. There were bottles of pills and a bottle of alcohol laying on the floor beside her, and her dad had run in after hearing her shouting at her to wake up.

Chloe had not really understood it all properly at the time as she was so young and her dad Richard had tried to protect her as best that he could, but as she had started to grow up, she could never shake the feeling of how much pain her mum must have been in to feel that she had no other option at all, other than to end her life and leave Chloe without her mum, who she adored and she knew her mum had felt the same. It still hurt every single day, no matter how many years went past.

She could still remember that exact moment, and how she felt once she knew that her mum was dead, it was still so clear and she would replay it in her mind, over and over again, and it would feel like she was right back there in that room seeing her mum on the sofa again and all those feelings would come flooding back and overwhelm her. It haunted her every day if she let it, but just a few months after her mum's death, her best friend Scarlett had lost her dad Matthew in a car accident. They only lived a few doors down from each other, and were friends even at that age, so when tragedy struck, she had someone there that knew exactly how she felt, and she didn't feel quite so alone even though they were both so devastated to have lost a parent, they loved so much and even at such a young age, they still looked after each other, comforted each other and they started to grow extremely close. They became each other's rocks and they had an unbreakable bond, not only in friendship but in their grief too, it had been such a harsh thing to go through when you are so young, but at least they had each other when they needed someone so badly and they were still best friends to this very day.

After Matthew had died the Fords moved house sadly, they simply couldn't face staying in the house after his death, they were still living fairly close by but it was not as close as they had been, which the girls missed a great deal. Richard and Chloe on the other hand had never even considered moving, as it would feel like they were leaving Elizabeth behind.

It had been so hard growing up without her mum, especially as she begun to hit big milestones in her life, it was a constant reminder that her mum wasn't there, she would never be there, she had missed everything and this made Chloe extremely angry at times, questioning how her mum could do that to her, she must have been so selfish to leave her all alone like that, maybe she didn't love Chloe as much as she thought, but deep down Chloe knew it wasn't that simple, her mum must have been going through something extremely difficult, and she knew in her heart that her mum MUST have really struggled to leave her behind. She just wished she could talk to her one last time and tell her how much she loved her.

Losing any parent is extremely tough so to have a friend who had lost her dad at a young age too, it helped in a weird way because they understood what each other was going through like no one else could, and they had each other to lean on when they needed it most. Chloe was so grateful to have Scarlett in her life, as well as her brother Sam and her mum Marie, as they had all rallied round and made sure everyone was ok under the circumstances, even though they were going through their own grief too they still took care of Chloe and her dad and the more time that Chloe and Scarlett spent together, they became the best of friends, real proper best friends and they loved each other very much. Chloe was grateful that she still had her dad but, he wasn't her mum and he was very protective of her, especially after her mum had passed away. He still struggled to talk about Elizabeth and Chloe would often catch him just staring at her photo, with a tear in his eye, he missed her as much as Chloe did, she could clearly see that. Richard had never really accepted what had happened, and he hadn't really been able to move on, he wouldn't even entertain the idea if Chloe ever suggested it, he would just say he didn't need anyone, but Chloe was worried about him, she felt that he was lonely and she knew she wouldn't always be around to keep him company and she didn't want him to be on his own.

Chloe had recently started dating Sam, who was Scarlett's slightly older brother, he was so sexy and handsome and had definitely got better looking as they had got older, people use to think he was a bit skinny at school and use to call him weedy but he had filled out a bit since then, he had even got himself a few tattoos which Chloe really liked and he was now an apprentice at a local building firm so he was gaining muscle all the time and he was starting to become more defined as he had also started going to the gym a couple of times a week, she sometimes wondered if this was so he didn't appear weak in front of her dad or so that he could protect her, she wasn't complaining though because he was absolutely gorgeous and she felt very lucky that they were together, and she looked forward to their future together, as Sam dreamed of the day when he would be a fully qualified builder and could build a family home for them one day, but she was always a little nervous that he would leave her one day, was their love true? It felt like it was but it didn't stop her constantly worrying that one day this would all be over, which is not what she wanted.

Chloe really had thought that everyone would be happy for them, especially Scarlett, as what more could you want, other than your best friend dating your brother, as that meant that one day, they could be sisters-in-law, but it was not a happy time at all, as for some reason Scarlett didn't seem to be pleased and her behaviour started to change, she was slowly starting to become a girl that Chloe did not really recognise anymore, her behaviour was changing and so was her appearance, she had dyed her hair black and was wearing more make up and she had even got herself a tattoo on the side of her neck and her nose pierced, she looked more like a goth than the girl she use to be, she was hanging around with new people that neither Chloe or Sam knew and she seemed extremely distant with everyone, even angry at times and she wouldn't talk to anyone at all, not even Chloe and she didn't know why, they use to tell each other everything, when did that change? had Chloe been too distracted with Sam and missed something? She felt guilty as she knew that since dating Sam, she had spent a lot of time with him, and she had not seen Scarlett very much, not like they would have seen each other before, she knew she wasn't being a very good friend right now and worried she had upset Scarlett.

Chloe had started to think about the past a lot recently, and about the good old days, when they were all younger and didn't feel like they had the weight of the world on their shoulders. She decided to go through all her old school stuff which she still had packed away, up in the loft. She wanted to see if she could find any old pictures of her and Scarlett that she might still have, any old letters or movie tickets - anything she could use to make a memory book of their friendship and give to Scarlett to remember they had a friendship worth saving, and that Chloe wasn't going anywhere, she would not give up on her no matter how hard she tried to push her away and hopefully the book would also act as a "I'm sorry" present too.

She had tried several times to talk to Scarlett, she thought being best friends meant they would always tell each other everything for the rest of their lives, but these days Scarlett just seemed to always brush Chloe off by saying she was fine which Chloe didn't believe was true. Their relationship had changed over the years but up until now, everything had still seemed to be ok between them, they never really fell out or argued, never really ever shouted at each other or had a crossed word to say, they had a true unbreakable friendship, that most friends could only dream about having.

Scarlett had recently got herself a job in a local bar and this seemed to coincide with the changes in her behaviour, appearance and attitude. Chloe wondered if maybe she was tired from working at night which she wasn't use to, or was she possibly annoyed that she had no choice but to get a job as she needed the money, and maybe she didn't really enjoy the job but knew she had no choice as Marie didn't seem to want to support her very much, Or maybe it was just a phase, like most people seem to go through at some point in their life, Chloe had certainly been through one a couple of years ago when she died her hair blue and had a fake nose piercing, thankfully it didn't last long. Chloe just didn't know what was going on with Scarlett anymore, and considering everything that had gone on between them since they were 6, Chloe couldn't understand why Scarlett would just stop talking to her like this and she was really worried that something wasn't right and she knew she needed to find out exactly what was going on before it got any worse.

She slowly started to open the box, preparing herself for what she might find inside, she hadn't looked at this stuff for a very long time and she knew there would be things reminding her of her mum still in there. She could not help missing that part of her life when everything had seemed to be more simple, when she and Scarlett really were true best friends and were having the time of their lives, they had been through so much and had a bond unlike anything else and that had always just made them stronger until now, Chloe was racking her brains trying to work out what was wrong.

Had something happened when they were growing up that Chloe had simply forgotten? Or maybe she had done or said something recently to upset Scarlett? She was sure that she would remember, but then she was so distracted by Sam lately, maybe that was the problem?

As she started to look back through her old diaries and photos she remembered something that had happened when they were about 16 and they were at a school disco she had been trying to push the memory to the back of her mind ever since it happened because it had been something that Chloe didn't want to remember or talk about as she remembered it all again now, it still felt a little uncomfortable, because at that particular moment, she had been SO embarrassed. What had Scarlett been thinking, trying to kiss her in front of everyone? It would not have been so bad if they had been on their own, but the whole school saw.

Chloe did not feel that way about Scarlett, at least not that night anyway, in that moment of time that is how she felt and she could still remember how she felt as she turned to see everyone looking at them, pointing and calling them lesbians and laughing at them, Chloe had gone bright red and ran out of the room, she realised she was going red again now as she recalled the memory although a lot had happened since that night, so there was a part of her that was blushing slightly now.

Scarlett had convinced her that it was just a joke but it hadn't felt that way to Chloe, it had not been funny at all to kiss her in front of everyone but also, it was a pretty good kiss for someone who was just "joking" and Chloe had kissed her back just for a moment, and had actually enjoyed it which she wasn't sure how she felt about that, it freaked her out so she had quickly pulled away.

She had not really been bothered by the kiss itself, it was more that it hadn't been private and it had never happened before so it was a pretty big thing to do at a school disco when they were not on their own, but Chloe knew she wasn't going to go down that road, she didn't want to explore what being with a girl was like and at that time, she was already starting to get close to Sam so it had been a very confusing time for her, but now she thought about it, Scarlett's behaviour did start to change a little bit after that night, and selfishly she had never really thought about how scarlett might have really be feeling, maybe she had been confused too? Did she say all that stuff just to make me feel better?

Or to throw me off if she did feel something for me? She wished now, that she had dealt with it better than she did, but she couldn't change that now, she just had to work out how to sort things out better this time.

She packed everything away back into the box again and decided that she was just going to have to meet up with Scarlett, whether she wanted to to or not and she would have it out with her, putting everything on the table, and hopefully get her talking. She would try her hardest to fix things between them once and for all, no matter how hard it might be, or embarrassing or even stressful it might be, because it simply couldn't go on any longer than it had already. She'd, had enough now, she had Sam but she wanted her best friend back, and he wanted his sister back too. Chloe just wanted everything to be just like it used to be, even though she knew that was not going to be quite as possible anymore.

Chapter Two

Scarlett was just a few weeks younger than Chloe and because they had known each other pretty much their whole lives and been through all the things that they had together, Scarlett felt that Chloe was the most important person in her life apart from her brother Sam. She had a non-existent relationship with her mum and she had no more family to speak of apart from her beloved grandad who was sadly now in a care home with extremely poor eye sight and hearing. Scarlett would often visit him and just sit with him so he wasn't alone, and she would draw a heart with her finger on the palm of his hand so that he knew it was Scarlett that was there with him.

When her dad passed away, her relationship with her mum became even worse and she would spend a lot of time with her grandparents, who were Matthews parents, she didn't know her other grandparents as they had given her mum away at birth and she had spent her life in care, maybe that explained some of her behaviour towards Scarlett, she was damaged by her own upbringing. Marie was not happy about Scarlett spending so much time at her grandparents' house and laughed at her when she asked if she could live with them, saying "do you really think they want you, don't you think they have been through enough without having you to deal with" she was so venomous when she spoke to Scarlett sometimes and she remembered running upstairs shouting back how much she hated her mum. All she wanted was to be closer to her real family, she missed her dad so much and so did her grandparents but they loved Scarlett and were nice to her, unlike her mum. Sadly not long after Matthew's death, his mum, Scarlett's nan suddenly passed away too, it was like she just couldn't carry on living anymore and just gave up, it was such an awful time. After that Marie banned Scarlett from going to their house saying her grandad needed time to grieve and that they should leave him alone, but Scarlett didn't believe that's what he wanted at all and she would sneak to his house after school and he was always so happy to see her and they would sit and talk for ages as Marie never seemed to care what time Scarlett came home, he confirmed her suspicions as he didn't want to be on his own and loved having Scarlett go and see him, he never understood why Marie was trying to keep them apart, after everything they had been through, they needed each other but she seemed determined to make everyone's lives miserable like hers, he had had never really like her, and liked her even less now, and he only cared about Sam and Scarlett.

As well as trying to deal with everything that was going on with her family and home life, Scarlett was also trying to deal with a secret that she was keeping, it was a big secret that no one else knew…. She was head over heels in love with Chloe and always had been, but after that night at the school disco, Scarlett's confidence had been shattered into a million pieces, she thought Chloe felt the same, but after they kissed it didn't feel like she did feel the same, so she had quickly deflected, saying it was a joke, she liked boys etc but Chloe HAD kissed her back, however brief it might have been surely it meant maybe, just maybe there might have been something there. She felt utterly confused and she also had her suspicions that her brother Sam might have something to do with it, and she was right as Chloe and Sam were now together, it had felt like a physical kick to the stomach when she found out and it was like her whole world had ended right there and then, why Chloe of all the girls in the world Sam could have picked!

Sam was always getting whatever he wanted ever since they were little and Scarlett always came second best, she had known from a young age that she had been an accident, and after her dads death she never felt like she was as loved by her mum, Marie not like Sam was and having both lost a parent, who they had loved so much, that's what brought her and Chloe closer together, because they both knew exactly what it was like to have your whole world change and come crashing down around you, knowing there was nothing you could ever do to change it, the ones they had lost, were never coming back and they had barely had a chance to get to know them, but now Sam was in the picture and he was going to get in the way, it wasn't fair why did he ALWAYS get what he wanted? What was SO special about him?! Didn't Scarlett deserve to be happy too? Most of her diary entries were all about her hate for Marie, how she wished Sam had never been worn and how all she wanted was Chloe, she was so angry about everything.

Scarlett had been really close to her brother when they were younger, and especially when their dad Matthew died, Sam knew what he needed to do and quickly stepped up and started to help take care of Scarlett even though he was not that much older than her, he was a great big brother, the best anyone could ask for, but as they got older Scarlett could clearly see the favouritism that their mum showed Sam and although she had tried her hardest not to let it get to her, it did and it hurt a LOT. This pain and sadness inside her slowly started to turn to anger and resentment over the years, and she started to blame Sam for everything, because if he wasn't here then Marie would love her more and she believe Chloe would too.

It was just the same thing time and time again, her mum just didn't seem to have any time for her or even want to be near her at times, it was always about Sam and no one else! When he needed to buy his first car, mum brought him one without any question, but when Scarlett needed a car Marie told her there wasn't enough money left so she would have to share Sam's car if he let her or she would have to share with her mum, surely when you have 2 children you try to treat them fairly and allow them to both have nice things but NO not for

Scarlett, she felt completely invisible and un-important to Marie she was sure that her mum probably wished she had never been born.

Even at bedtime, Marie still treated them differently, it was like she just couldn't or didn't know how to love Scarlett at all, not even a little bit and it upset Scarlett so much, she spent so many nights crying into her pillow so no one would hear her and then falling asleep, all she wished was that her dad was there to make everything better. Marie would quickly tuck Scarlett in and simply say goodnight, no kisses or cuddles and she would be left to read a book by herself, but when it came to Sam she would go in and sit with him, cuddling him, talking to him, reading him a story, telling him how much she loved him, why couldn't they do all that together, why was Scarlett always left out? Did Marie not realise that Scarlett could see and hear what was going on, was she doing it on purpose, like some sort of punishment? What had Scarlett ever done that was so bad that her mum didn't love her? could she not see how upset it made her?

She remembered stories Sam would tell her about how Marie would always pick him up from school without fail what and she would hold his hand and ask about how his day had been, how she would sit with him and help him with his homework, no matter what, she ALWAYS had time for him and would help him any way she could with whatever he needed help with, but when it was Scarlett's turn to do those things, if she was lucky Marie would pick her up, but often it was Ir child's mum and this was only until she was the age where she could walk home by herself and then she was left to walk home alone even though she would walk Sam home right up until he left primary school.   When it came to her homework, all she ever got from her mum was "Ask Your brother" or "I am too busy" she never tried to even find 1 minute for Scarlett, she just wasn't interested and gradually as Scarlett got older she realised just how she was being treated by her mum and was REALLY starting to get fed up of it, she had done nothing wrong and she wasn't going to put up with it for much longer.

She had doted on her dad Matthew SO much, he never treated her like her mum did and it helped to balance it out, Scarlett was happy when she was with her dad and it hurt so much to lose him at such a young age, she hardly got any time with him, and then she had been left with her awful mum, why did he have to die, why couldn't it have been her or even Sam!

She did care about her family, after all, they were all she had apart from Chloe, there was no one else and she was not very good at making new friends. She tried her best to get on with life and not let things bother her too much, she knew she couldn't change the past but she could have a say in how her future turned out. She would try and help her mum around the house and do things like the food shopping for her, the gardening, the cleaning etc, anything Marie couldn't do, didn't want to do or didn't have time to do, and Scarlett had hoped for a while that it might start to make her mum notice her more and maybe show her a bit more love but she was wrong as it never seemed to change a single thing and as time went on she realised that things were just never ever going to change, she decided she needed a new life away from her family, just her and Chloe, they could go travelling or move somewhere far away from here, and far away from everyone she hated and they could be really happy together, away from everyone else, there was just two problems…. One was Convincing Chloe and the other was getting rid of Sam.

Chapter Three

Scarlett could still remember the exact moment when she realised she loved Chloe, in more than just a friends kind of way and it had never scared or worried her that she was in love with a girl, she had felt this way for so long that it felt completely normal to her, but she knew that other people might not be so understanding and that even Chloe herself might be a bit surprised and need some time to get her head around it all.

They had been about 10 years old and there was a group of them at someone's house, it hadn't been someone that Chloe and Scarlett were great friends with but there had been a bunch of girls that had just started hanging around with each other at school and one of them said they could come over for a sleep over, so once Chloe had said yes, then Scarlett was in as well, since she was her best friend, and they hardly ever did anything without each other. They were staying downstairs in the living room, they were laughing and talking, they had a movie marathon and lots of food and fizzy drinks, they were all loving life right there in that moment, it was great. They snuggled down to watch the last film and Chloe laid her head in Scarlett's arms, Scarlett just looked down at her to see her watching the film, smiling and looking so content she just couldn't take her eyes off her and suddenly her heart skipped a beat and that was the moment she realised it was so much more than just friendship for her and it cemented any suspicions she had already had about how she felt.

She had always been a bit unsure whether she actually liked girls or even boys OR was it just Chloe, she assumed to start with that it was normal that as you were growing up and trying to figure life out that this might be another thing you had to work out but she knew that she had always had stronger feelings for Chloe than anyone else but this was surely understandable considering what they had both been through growing up together, no matter what, all that Scarlett did know was there was something special about Chloe, and she wanted more.

Those feelings had never left Scarlett, every time she saw Chloe, her heart would beat faster, she would get a dry mouth and just wanted to tell her how she felt but she was never brave enough in case Chloe didn't feel the same and that would have been the end of her fantasy. She didn't want to lose her but Chloe was starting to show interest in boys, nothing serious but there were a few boyfriends at school and Scarlett was so jealous, she wanted to be the one Chloe chose but how could she be, when she didn't know how Scarlett really felt about her?

Scarlett had pictures of Chloe on the inside of her wardrobe and there were diaries for every year, all with details of how she felt about Chloe, she was definitely the ONE! It was like being a teenager again with boyband posters on your walls and a diary that you wrote every little thing in, she was totally 100% in love with Chloe and wanted to be with her SO badly it actually hurt, it was like her life depended on Chloe loving her back otherwise she would die and the inside of her wardrobe was starting to become a shrine to Chloe, she kept everything from cinema tickets to letters and even receipts from places they had been together, even the shops and she was becoming a bit obsessed, ALWAYS checking to see what she was posting on her social media, and she had even followed her sometimes without her knowing, her feelings for Chloe were extremely deep routed and she couldn't think about anything else, other than being with the girl she loved and REALLY wanted to be hers and no one elses!

She couldn't help thinking back to that awful night though, the night that had started with so much hope and excitement. The day of the school disco had been looming, and Scarlett had decided that the disco was going to be the place, where she would tell Chloe how she finally felt, she was nervous but knew if she could pull this off, then it would be the start of a beautiful happily ever after life for her and Chloe, one that Scarlett had been dreaming about for a very long time.

The night itself had started well, they decided they would get ready at Scarlett's house, the music was on loud, they were dancing, smiling and having fun, it was like they had no cares in the world at all, the atmosphere was so joyful, but inside Scarlett's insides were in knots and she felt sick with nerves but she didn't let Chloe see that. Seeing how happy Chloe looked just made Scarlett smile, it could finally be the night that she got the girl of her dreams and she couldn't wait!

The disco was in full flow, everyone was having a great time on the dance floor, it felt like the first chance to let their hair down at 16 with no parents around before being old enough to go clubbing or drinking without any chaperones at all.

It was coming towards the end of the night and the typical "slow" song came on, as neither Chloe or Scarlett were going out with anyone at that time and they had gone to the disco together, they had decided that they would dance to this song together so that they didn't have to sit out and watch everyone else doing it and as best friends it didn't feel strange to do this, and it gave Scarlett the perfect opportunity.

The song started and they put their arms around each other, looking around to see what everyone else was doing, they looked at each other and both burst out laughing. They started to dance and inside Scarlett was feeling more and more nervous, she felt like she couldn't focus properly and her legs felt weak she needed to tell Chloe right away, but in a split second what she actually decided to do was to lean in and kiss Chloe and in that moment, Scarlett felt completely elated, it was literally everything she had always dreamt about, she was finally kissing the girl of her dreams and that girl was kissing her back, or so she thought, it was only for a split second, and then it was over just as quickly as it had begun. Scarlett was worried as to how Chloe would react, this was such a big deal for Scarlett and she really hoped she hadn't blown her chance.

Chloe may have for that moment kissed Scarlett back but she had pulled away pretty quick and had not seemed happy at all, saying to Scarlett

"What do you think you are doing"

She had looked around at everyone else who had seen what had happened and were now pointing at them and whispering, Chloe had run out of the room, Scarlett had gone after her inside her heart was beating so fast and she could feel tears pricking her eyes.

When they both got outside Scarlett found herself apologising, she didn't want to apologise, she didn't feel she had anything to apologise for but she could see that Chloe was upset and that had not been her intention at all.

She had managed (she thought) to convince Chloe it had just been a moment of madness, that she got carried away with the dancing and the music and of course she wasn't gay, it was just a bit of fun and that she was very sorry. Chloe seemed to just about buy the excuse, not that she seemed any happier, they both just wanted to go home, so Scarlett rang her brother Sam and asked him if he could pick them up. While they waited they sat on a bench near the carpark, in total silence, not looking at each other, but Scarlett kept trying to look at Chloe from the corner of her eye, she really thought that Chloe felt the same, and she couldn't shake the thought because she HAD kissed her back, but right now she felt really sad and very worried about what would happen next.

She had never EVER imagined being with anyone else, what would she do now? what would happen to them as friends, she couldn't lose Chloe. She just wanted to cry and was trying really hard not too in front of Chloe as she didn't want her to see that she was upset otherwise her story wouldn't add up, but it was like Chloe instinctively knew Scarlett needed her and she reached across and held her hand in hers, still not saying anything, and still looking ahead but it was that little bit of intimacy and kindness that Scarlett needed in that moment and it made her realise this wasn't the end, she wasn't going to give up, she would make Chloe see that they were meant to be together, no matter what and she just sat there and enjoyed that moment alone together before Sam turned up.

When he arrived, Chloe got in the front, and Sam asked if they were both ok, they said yes but didn't want to talk as they were tired, Sam wondered if they were telling the truth as neither of them looked very happy and it felt a bit tense as well. As they were driving back home Scarlett noticed that Sam and Chloe kept looking at each other and she was sure she saw Sam mouth "are you sure you are ok" to Chloe and that Chloe nodded, it seemed a bit strange but then they were all friends and Sam would see Scarlett when they got home so maybe he was just asking and nothing else, but Scarlett did feel a bit jealous, maybe more because the night had not quite gone the way that she had intended it to.

After that night, things had been strained for quite a while between Chloe and Scarlett and Chloe also started hanging around with Sam more and more which she didn't like very much, it felt a bit weird knowing they were spending so much time together without her, but then Scarlett had met Pixie who started at her work as the new bar manager, she just walked in one day and Scarlett couldn't take her eyes of her, she was stunning and they hit it off straight away, and it felt really refreshing, it was new, exciting and different, not long after meeting each other they started dating.

Pixie was never going to be a replacement for Chloe but it allowed her to take her mind off things, relax and just have a bit of fun again, which she felt she had been missing for a while. Pixie was gorgeous, so funny and easy going, she would be most girls or guys dreams and Scarlett fancied her a lot and was really enjoying spending time with her, but she just wasn't Chloe and they both knew that. She just wanted to block out her feelings for Chloe, she wanted her more than anything else in the world but it felt like it was becoming clear that Chloe didn't feel the same way. Scarlett needed time to work out her feelings and what if anything she could do to eventually be with Chloe. Pixie was a distraction, but she also allowed to her explore her sexuality more, she had still not wanted to be openly gay and Sam and Marie didn't know either, and she certainly hadn't wanted Chloe to know, not yet, Chloe was everything to her and she needed to get this right if she was ever going to win over the girl of her dreams.

She was having lots of fun with Pixie and it had definitely made things clear in Scarlett's mind that it was Girls she liked, not boys but

Pixie was not the one for her, not her soul mate or the one she wanted to settle down with one day, and Pixie knew that but for now, was happy to just have a bit of fun. Scarlett's best friend Josh who was also a friend of Pixies and worked at the same pub they did, agreed he would act as her pretend "boyfriend" as and when she needed it, to help keep her secrets safe, it was the perfect cover for her. They all worked together and were great friends too so it worked really well.

For some reason, everyone seemed to think that Scarlett wasn't ok, that her behaviour was different, which it was but she couldn't see what the problem was. She was young, and care free, and she was just trying to enjoy her life whilst also trying to not think about Chloe ALL the time but Chloe was starting to seriously mess with her mind and she was annoyed that everyone thought there was something wrong with her, when it was Chloe who was starting to act differently and spending more time with Sam instead of her, her best friend.

Chloe was the one that wanted to up and leave everyone behind and start a new life with Sam, shouldn't people be more worried about that?

Chloe had told her that it felt like she was being pushed away, that she cares about her more than she realises and she doesn't want to lose her but this just made Scarlett feel more frustrated because she just didn't seem to have a clue how Scarlett was really feeling, and it was Chloe's behaviour that was causing the problem, so this wasn't helping at all but she had tried to be as honest as she thought she could be, telling Chloe.

"You are not losing me, you could never loose me, I love you" Scarlett hugged her and took a deep breath to smell her hair and perfume without her noticing. I'm ok honestly I am being careful, mum always knows where I am when I am out and I always come home alone so you don't need to worry about me, ok"

Scarlett felt like she was not being completely honest, as she wasn't having quite as much fun as she was making out to everyone, she was hurting, she wanted Chloe so badly but just didn't know how to tell her. The last time she had tried at the school disco, had not gone well and it had taken a long time for Scarlett to deal with that rejection and even contemplate trying again, but she hated seeing Chloe with Sam. How could Chloe not realise how much Scarlett really loved her? They had always been so close, and that had been ok up to now but it wasn't enough anymore, she needed Chloe to be hers. She wanted more and she needed more too, no more messing around or playing it safe, too much had happened between them and she wanted to sort things out once and for all with Chloe.

As they began getting older there were several moments if they were out and drunk that Chloe would tell her she loved her and kiss her, more than just a quick peck and there had been another occasion where they had shared a proper full on kiss, they had gone back to Scarlett's, both got undressed and into bed that night they did things

that they had never done with each other before –
Scarlett had been waiting for that moment her
whole life and couldn't believe it was actually
happening, but the next morning Chloe had acted
like nothing had happened between them, she
didn't acknowledge ANY of it, Scarlett couldn't
work out if she genuinely couldn't remember, had
she really drink that much? or was she trying to
wipe it from her memory? Scarlett was starting to
feel that Chloe was clearly a bit confused but if she
was aware of any of she was doing, then she was
playing with Scarlett's emotions and that wasn't
fair, she needed to ask her what was going on, even
though she was as nervous as hell, in case Chloe
said something she didn't want to hear

Chloe didn't seem to know what Scarlett meant,
so she explained it all to her, reminding her of
exactly what had happened, Chloe admitted that
she did remember but she didn't want to admit to
herself that she had feelings for Scarlett she just
wanted to have a bit of fun and had assumed that
Scarlett was ok with that.

Scarlett was honest with her, she felt like she had nothing to lose anymore and she told her she had broken her heart the night of the disco but Chloe was confused because she thought they had dealt with that, plus Scarlett had a boyfriend, what about Josh?

Scarlett had to explain that Josh was gay, he wasn't her boyfriend, he was helping her to cover up a relationship she was having with Pixie because she didn't know if she was ready for everyone to know she was gay.

She was very careful not to declare her undying love for Chloe right there and then as she didn't want to blow her chances, if she was ever going to get Chloe to realise she was gay too, things needed to be done cautiously so that she didn't scare her off.

Chloe tried to apologise, she admitted she was confused about her feelings but she really liked a boy she had met so knew that she liked boys and therefore she had convinced herself that she must be straight, because if she wasn't how could she feel the way she did about him?

Scarlett felt so frustrated, telling Chloe that she could like both girls and boys! but who was this mystery boy Chloe was talking about as she hadn't mentioned anyone, the only boy she ever saw her with most of the time was Sam....

She had frozen, not able to speak, she looked at Chloe and could just tell from her face expression that it was Sam, what a total nightmare, why Sam, why her brother of all the people she could have chosen to go out with, she wanted to scream.

Chloe tried to make things better saying she should have told Scarlett sooner, she was sorry, she didn't know how she would react and she wasn't ready for everyone to know about them yet but then she had started to have having feelings for Scarlett as well, and felt very confused, she started to cry, Scarlett just walked up to her, placed a hand either side of her face and kissed her, Chloe kissed her back and it was amazing. Scarlett told her not to worry, that it would all be ok, she promised.

That had been the start of things, from that moment on, they had started to have an affair, Chloe knew this wasn't fair to Sam but she couldn't let either of them go, she loved them both so much and they both made her really happy she couldn't imagine not having either of them in her life but she knew it wasn't right to be with them both at the same time but she wasn't ready to choose between them.

Scarlett wanted more, she didn't care about Sam, she was finally with Chloe and it was just a matter of time before she would be all hers and no one else's but she knew that Sam would be an obvious problem and that potentially Chloe would never let him go, certainly not very easily anyway, so she needed to work out a way that Sam would be the one to walk away from Chloe. Maybe she could try to find another girl that he might like, and convince him to go on a date? no, that wouldn't work, she knew he would never do that to Chloe "damn it" she thought it needed to be something bigger than that, he needs to be completely out of the picture somehow, it was something she would need to think about a bit more but for now, she was just enjoying finally being with Chloe every chance she had, she loved Chloe so much it hurt and she missed her as soon as she wasn't with her anymore, it was like movie love, she was addicted, it was like Chloe was a drug, that she just couldn't get enough of.

As for Pixie, she was fully aware of what was going on, she always had been. They had both always been really honest with each other right since the very start of their relationship and she had been ok with that until mow as she had slowly started to wish she was the one that Scarlett wanted so badly, she could only imagine what love like that would feel like, they got on really well and were having a great time, and sometimes, just sometimes, Chloe was not always the topic of conversation which was nice

She saw another side to Scarlett, that not many other people seemed to ever see, there was a vulnerability there, that she suspected Scarlett didn't let anyone else see and she could really imagine them being a proper couple, helping her to come out as gay to everyone, and really being happy together, she wanted them to be together properly but she knew that she would never be the one for Scarlett no matter whether she tried to talk to her about it or not.

She had spoken to her a few times before but just knew there was no chance at all, for them and she just had to accept that, because if she didn't, then she would lose Scarlett altogether and she wasn't ready to stop things between them, and felt that just some of Scarlett was better than none of her at all but if Scarlett really did want Chloe and no one else, then she wished that they would just be honest with themselves, sort things out between them and finally tell the world, no more secrets, no more lies because that never leads to anything good in the end and she knew that eventually, that someone would have their heart broken.

Chapter Four

When Scarlett wasn't thinking about Chloe or Pixie she was at home trying to do her best to help her mum around the house, even though her mum never seemed to notice or appreciate it, she felt like she needed to try and be the best daughter she could be. Was she trying to get attention from her mum or did she hope this would make her mum love her? Scarlett really wasn't sure anymore.

She had spent SO much of her life fighting to be noticed by her mum, as well as Chloe in some respects and she was starting to feel more and more fed up each day and these feelings of sadness and pain were slowly starting to develop into hate and anger towards her mum, but for now she decided that she would carry on doing her bit in the house, she didn't want to give her mum any excuse to be unpleasant to her, her brother Sam on the other hand seemed to be spending more and more time out of the house to be with Chloe and it was so frustrating because not only was he with Chloe, even if he did nothing at all around the house, he could do no wrong in mums eyes, she never said anything, or even asked him to help with anything. Scarlett could see how his good looks had won Chloe over, as he was a good looking boy but what was so special about him in their mums eyes apart from being the first child to be born.

It was a crisp and cold Monday morning, both Marie and Sam had left to go to work and Scarlett didn't work on Mondays. Marie had appeared to be getting a bit sentimental over the weekend as it had been the anniversary of Matthews death and she had got the family memory box out, but she wouldn't let Sam and Scarlett look through the box together, without her and she insisted on keeping it on her knee and only picked a few select things out to let them see.

Scarlett wanted more, she missed her dad SO much and as she got older, the memories of him seemed to be fading as she had been so young when he died, she had an idea of where her mum kept the memory box so now she was in the house alone she decided to see if she could find it, she just wanted to see what else was in there of her dads, she wanted to feel close to him, she still felt the pain she did the day he died, it hurt so much and Marie almost seemed to pretend he didn't exist anymore or that he didn't still need to be remembered by them all. She understood that people grieve in different ways and often want to bury painful memories but she didn't, she wanted to talk about him and keep his memory alive and she wondered if there might have been something in that box that Marie couldn't bear to look at or show to them of her dads, Scarlett wanted to see it all.

Upstairs in her mums bedroom, she found the box on the top shelf of her double wardrobe, it was pushed right to the back and hidden under a large green and red checked blanket, was her mum trying to hide it? she wondered, or maybe it still brought back bad memories for her and she needed to keep it out of sight? Marie hardly ever talked about Matthew anymore and it made Scarlett feel sad, it was like her mum didn't want to remember him, but he hadn't just been her husband, he had been Sam and Scarlet's dad, and he was still their dad it didn't matter that he wasn't psychically there anymore as Scarlett believed she could feel his presence sometimes and it was comforting to her to believe it, even if no one else did.

She sat on the floor, with her back against the radiator, it was still warm from the heating being on that morning and made her feel relaxed and soothed just for a second, she did feel a bit guilty going through something so personal, even if it was her mum's stuff and as soon as she lifted the lid off the box she questioned whether she should really be doing this, what if she found something she didn't really want to see, or shouldn't see? but they were not just her mums memories, she had a right to know more about her dad and if Marie wasn't going to show her or tell her more, then she needed to find out for herself.

Her breathing was starting to get heavier and her mouth was drying up, she felt anxious as she looked down at her mums diary and it felt like a massive invasion of privacy but she just couldn't stop herself from picking it up and opening it to read.

On the inside of the front cover was a picture of them as a family - all 4 of them, and tears pricked Scarlett's eyes, she sat there for what felt like a lifetime just staring at that photo, they all looked so happy and she just wanted things to be like that again. She slowly started to turn the pages and she suddenly spotted Richard, Chloe's dads name and wondered if there would be anything about Chloe in there, but she was quickly shocked out of that thought by what she read......

"I saw Richard again tonight, I feel so guilty doing this behind Elizabeth's back, but I love him so much and he loves me, Matthew doesn't care about me anymore, he is never here and he is oblivious that this is going on behind his back"

Scarlett's mouth fell open, she was staring at the words on the page, her eyes quickly reading the words over and over again, had she really just read that? She shut the diary and laid it on the floor, she closed her eyes hoping it would have disappeared by the time she opened them again, she slowly opened her eyes again and could feel tears falling down her cheeks as she looked down, the diary was still there, she took a deep breath and tried to wipe her tears away with the sleeve of her jumper, she picked the diary back up, and opened it once more and began reading again, she REALLY didn't want to read anymore, but felt compelled to know more and she couldn't stop herself.

"Oh my god, I think I might be pregnant! I don't know what to do, I know 100% that it's not Matthews, but Richard has already said he can't and won't leave Elizabeth. She is my best friend and I never meant to hurt her, but I just can't stop how I feel about Richard. I'm going to have to tell him, but I'm scared as to what will he say, I really hope he won't be too angry with me"

"Matthew knows everything, I couldn't keep it from him anymore, how was I supposed to hide a baby from him? Richard said he still loves me, and will help me where he can but he just cannot leave Elizabeth, he loves her too much and they are trying for a baby themselves, it hurts so much that I am not the one he wants but I know I can't do this all on my own so I decided to tell Matthew everything in the hope he would stay with me, he was obviously extremely shocked, upset and angry and it was horrible to see him crying, but he told me he actually felt guilty, he hadn't been here enough or paid me enough attention and he loved me, he couldn't be without me and we could make

this work. I feel so relieved, if the baby is a boy, we are going to call him Sam after Matthews grandad. Maybe If I'm really careful, I might even be able to still see Richard"

Scarlett could not believe what she was reading, what the hell was her mum thinking convincing dad to look after Sam but still hoping to carry on her affair with Richard, how could she do that to him? If she didn't already hate her mum, she did now more than ever before.

"Oh my god, Elizabeth has just told me she is pregnant, and I've found out I'm pregnant again too, it hurts so much to know she is having Richards baby and they can be a real family together, I don't want this baby, I had 1 stupid fumbled night with Matthew, I don't want another baby, I don't want Matthews baby, I want Richards baby, this is SO messed up I really don't know what to do, I can't bring myself to get rid of the baby, but I feel hatred towards it already and it

hasn't even be born yet, I'm a horrible person, it's no wonder Richard doesn't want me anymore"

"I just can't believe it.... Elizabeth is dead! Richard said she had found out about their affair and somehow worked out that Sam was his child not Matthews, they argued and he stormed out of the house to go and get Chloe from school, but when they got back, the house was very quiet and Chloe went to find her mum and found her in the living room, and all Richard heard was Chloe shouting "mummy wake up" he ran into the room and saw Elizabeth lying on the sofa. He said it looked like she had taken an overdose, as there was packets of all sorts of tablets and alcohol laying on the floor, he checked for her pulse and couldn't feel one so he rang an ambulance and just sat there waiting for them to arrive, with Chloe in his arms. It must have been so awful for them both, I feel like this is ALL my fault, I don't even know how I can begin to start making this right, I just can't believe she's dead, how could I do this to my best friend"

Scarlett felt sick, she leant her head back against the radiator and closed her eyes, she was trying to control her breathing to stop herself feeling sick but it wasn't working, tears were falling down her cheeks uncontrollably and she was struggling to process everything she had just read, how could they do that to Elizabeth, or Matthew, all the lies and the all secrets, she could feel the anger rising inside her, was this why she didn't love Scarlett as much as Sam, because she wasn't Richards baby too, and she had to stay with dad rather that living the life she really wanted with Richard? It all made sense now, but what was Scarlett supposed to do now?

Suddenly, she realised something and as she wiped her tears away and blew her nose, she started to feel calmer and an evil smile crept across her face, as she realised she now had the PERFECT reason to break Sam and Chloe up, because they were RELATED! This massive secret Maire had been keeping from everyone all this time, but that muse have meant that Richard knew as well, why did no one try stopping them getting together in the first place? She was confused, surely neither Marie or Richard wanted Sam and Chloe to be together when they KNEW they were related to each other?

What to do now though, she thought to herself… do I tell mum I know and then question her to get the answers I need? Do I Tell Richard I know and see how he reacts? Maybe I could start by telling Sam he needs to break up with Chloe, otherwise I will share a massive secret with everyone, that NOONE wants to be let out! Or do I let Chloe "accidently" find the diary so she finds out for herself? There were so many options one thing was for sure, Scarlett had some serious thinking to do, she didn't want to upset Chloe any more than was necessary, and she needed her to realise the Scarlett was the one she should be with, all in, forever, so whatever she did, Scarlett could not be found out by Chloe, she could not risk losing the love of her life, not now.

She took photos of as many pages as she could and put everything back exactly how she had found it, she didn't want her mum knowing she had found it, she would need to bide her time for now and work out what to do next, she would be with Chloe soon no matter what. This changes everything she thought, it's time to punish mum and Richard and teach them both a lesson. She still just could not believe what she had read but she did know that she felt very, very angry and was so upset now she knew how her mum and Richard had treated her Dad and Elizabeth and she needed to make them pay for what they had done, because of them all the children had grown up without a parent, and it was their fault!

Scarlett never thought it was possible that she could commit a crime, and certainly not murder, but you never really know what someone is capable of until they are pushed far enough, and in that moment Scarlett certainly considered killing her mum!

Thankfully for Scarlett, no one knew of her new developing dark intentions so she could almost do whatever she wanted if she knew she could get away with it this wasn't where she thought her life would take her, but she was happy to accept it, if it meant she could get the one thing she had wanted her whole life, more than anything else in the whole world....Chloe! It was all for Chloe and Scarlett was prepared to do whatever it took.

Chapter Five

I wish Scarlett would stop asking me about Matthew, I know he was her dad and she misses him but it is still incredibly painful for me, not only the sadness I feel, but the guilt I feel too and also the deep regret that I never end up with what I really wanted and I still blame Matthew for that even though he is no longer here and none of this was his fault, not really, we were just starting to drift apart and his work got in the way a lot of the time and I never tried to talk to him about it, or tried to really sort things out with him, which is what I should have done but instead I chose to have an affair with my best friends husband, Matthew and Elizabeth both deserved so much better than me and Richard maybe its karma that I was never able to have what I really wanted, it's my punishment for all the wrong that I have done and all the pain I have caused.

I never wanted another child but I couldn't bear to get rid of the baby, and Matthew had said it would all be ok, but it wasn't ok at all, because Matthew wasn't Richard, Sam wasn't even his son and all I ever wanted was to be with Richard and our baby boy Sam, so when Matthew died and I was then left completely on my own to look after 2 young children, one of which I didn't really want, I just wished Richard would come and rescue me, looking back I can't believe that I actually thought I still had a chance with him after Matthews death, like I had some kind of free pass now he was gone, how awful to even think like that.

It hurt so much to hear Richard say he was staying with Elizabeth even when I told him I was pregnant, they were apparently trying for a baby too and that was the end of our affair, albeit not for a while as we just couldn't keep away from each other. Matthew was so stupid he never suspected a thing, and he truly believed that Sam was his, so when Scarlett came long he thought our family was complete, but it wasn't what I wanted and that day he died was horrible, Elizabeth had not long committed suicide and everything came out, every little detail that had happened between me and Richard, he was so upset and really shouldn't have got in the car but he drove off and not long afterwards she had received the call to say he had been killed in a road traffic accident, he had veered across the road and hit another car head on, he was the only casualty, his death was my fault, I am a terrible person.

I decided to get the memory box out today to see if that would stop Scarlett asking so many questions, well that was a BIG mistake as I forgot my diary was in there and Scarlett just wanted to look through EVERYTHING! I was trying to keep it all on my knee so I could keep control of what she could and couldn't see, she has always been so difficult compared to Sam, far too strong minded and she always wanted to be with me growing up, she was clingy and felt like a burden to me, seeing her every day just reminded me that I didn't have Richard and I had lost Matthew, so I felt like I had no one to turn to and no one to love me or take care of me.

I resented her and I knew that I didn't love her half as much as I loved Sam, I'm sure that is part of the reason she is behaving the way she is now, and I don't really feel that I can say anything, how can I stop her living her life as she wants to when I couldn't love her enough as her mother, I have let her down so terribly, we are always snapping at each other and we argue a lot, I wish things could have been different, I really do but it's too late now, all I can do is learn to live under the safe roof as best we can together, it might not be too much longer before Scarlett decides to move out, Sam is already planning to move away with Chloe one day and I will be completely alone then, so I need to make sure I don't completely ruin my relationship with Scarlett, she will soon be all I have left even if we don't live together in the future.

She must think I am being funny with her all the time, but I just can't help it, I have never been able to help it, I do love her of course I do and I did love Matthew just not enough, and towards the end it was Richard I wanted more than anything else and I really thought having a baby would be the answer that would bring us together finally, not that it was planned of course, but it wasn't and look where we all are now, no one got what they wanted even after causing all that pain and suffering so was it really worth it in the end? I ask myself this all the time as Richard barely speaks to me anymore, I think his guilt has completely consumed him and he can't even bear to look at me, god knows what his feelings truly are for Sam knowing he is his son and the result of our affair.

I tried to kill myself at once, but I couldn't go through with it when it came to it, not after what had happened with Elizabeth, and I couldn't bear to leave Sam and Scarlett without a mum, even a rubbish mum, it would have been so selfish of me, I have to live with the pain as a punishment for what I've done, I also couldn't put them all through that kind of pain again, it wouldn't have been fair.

I have tried to protect Sam from all of this since he was born, he had no idea about what was going on when he was little but I just couldn't do the same for Scarlett, I would hold her as a baby and just cry because I felt guilty for not loving her as much as Sam, she felt like the reason I wasn't with Richard even though I know that isn't true, but having a baby with Matthew was never what I wanted and losing him in such a tragic accident, not long after Elizabeth took her own life had just been too much to deal with on my own, but Richard didn't want anything to do with me after that, no matter how much I tried. Eventually I just stopped trying but I miss him so much and I wish we could get back what we once had and be together again but I suppose that's not possible now Chloe and Sam are together. I still cannot believe they are together, why did neither me or Richard do something to stop it, we are complete idiots for letting this happen.

I can't believe I just sat there and smiled so much, when Sam and Chloe told us, because inside I felt like screaming but I just acted like it was the best news ever, I didn't even realise the words that were coming out of my mouth, Scarlett didn't look that happy for some reason, not sure what was up with her.

I had to quickly excuse myself and went upstairs, I couldn't help pacing the room as I started to panic. I couldn't believe this was happening, Sam was going out with Chloe, his half-sister, I had known they were close, but not that close, how did I not spot this sooner? What on earth was I going to do? I sat on the edge of my bed and thought about ringing Richard, but I knew I couldn't because I had not spoken to him for ages and it would be really awkward, but then this was really awkward too. I've always tried to protect Sam and Richard, but if this got out I didn't know that I could do that anymore, this could ruin everyone's lives, it would be history repeating itself all over again, but if it didn't come out, then how on earth would we be able to get them to split up? Because they can't continue being in a relationship with each other.

I had been upstairs a while and didn't want anyone worry about me, so I quickly washed my face, I could hear everybody downstairs laughing and talking, usually this would make me smile, but not that night.

I still keep an old photo in my bedside drawer, it is of me and Matthew with the kids and our neighbours at the time, Chloe, Elizabeth and Richard, we all look so happy and we had all been such good friends at the time, how did it go so horribly wrong, I couldn't help crying when I looked at this picture because I still mourn the life that I once had and that I know I will never get back, I also know that I will never stop feeling guilting for destroying everything.

I think when they first started getting a bit closer I just naively thought, let it run its course, it won't last forever but now they are talking about moving away and starting a family, I may have no other option to try and speak to Richard now as something needs to change and fast.

Chapter Six

Mum decided to get the memory box out yesterday for some reason, probably because Scarlett wants to know more about dad and asks a lot of questions about him, all the time, but mum seemed to be stopping us from looking through it by ourselves, as she kept it on her knee the whole time, she was acting a bit strange and was choosing certain things to show us, rather than letting us see it all, it is such a shame as Scarlett didn't get anywhere near as much time with dad as I did, and even my time wasn't that much, but I know how much it upsets her, even when she doesn't talk about it, I can still tell and all she wanted was to talk about him more and see more of his things that were in the memory box but mum wouldn't let her

Mum certainly behaved differently around Scarlett when we were growing up and I know I was still young myself so didn't really understand everything, but it definitely felt that I was the favourite, it was like mum loved me more than Scarlett and she didn't try and pretend otherwise. It felt like mum didn't want Scarlett at all, especially after losing dad, she would always be telling Scarlett "your brother can help you" or "go and do it yourself, you don't need any help" it just didn't feel like she cared about anything involving Scarlett, and she was always trying to pass her off onto other people, which is such an awful thing to say I know, but that's what it felt like. Mum was never like that with me though, so I have never understood why it was different with Scarlett

I use to try and do whatever I could to help make Scarlett feel happy and loved, it wasn't fair for her, she was just a little child. I loved, and still love having a little sister, someone to play with when we were younger, someone to look after but also annoy and we have got on so well as we have grown up, and I thought we were really close, but lately it has started to feel different, between us, I don't think she likes the fact that I now have a girlfriend especially as it is her best friend Chloe, she says she is happy for us but it doesn't feel like that, I thought Scarlett would love the fact that her best friend and brother were now together but I guess I didn't think about the effect it might have on their friendship, or ours for that matter.

We have all grown up together and have always got on so well, I just started to feel something a bit more for Chloe and, turns out that she felt the same, we didn't think we would be hurting anyone and certainly did not want to upset anyone, we are just 2 young people madly in love with each other but I guess it means both me and Chloe are now not spending as much time as we use to with Scarlett and I think she is maybe a bit lonely, as she doesn't have many friends, or not that I am aware of anyway, and how mum treated her and still treats her sometimes, must have an impact on her in all aspects of her life, I wish I had done more for her, I still don't know what to do now, I should have said something to Mum before but how could I ask her if she hated her own daughter? which is how it felt, I didn't want to do anything that would ruin my relationship with mum, which looking back was very selfish of me, I should have done something more to sort things out for Scarlett.

I have heard her arguing with mum recently and they snap at each other so much, Scarlett stays out lot and I think she is drinking too, she won't talk to anyone anymore, she just says she is ok and is enjoying her life, while she is still young. Chloe said she has a plan to try and get her talking so I really hope she opens up as we all want to make sure she is ok, we care about her and I miss her, I really want my little sister back. I always imagined when we got older and we both had partners that we could double date and still get on as well as we did when we were little, she is supposedly seeing this guy Josh but we have only ever seen a picture of him, and sometimes glimpsed him in the car when he comes to pick her up but no one seems to have ever actually seen him or met him properly, certainly not to talk to. Why hasn't she introduced him to anyone? she seems to like to keep her cards really close to her chest and only likes to let a few very selected people in, it's like she wants to keep everything to herself and doesn't want to share anything with us. She never talks about him, and says she doesn't want to bring him home to meet us, so it all feels a bit strange to me if I'm honest, what is the big deal? Is there something she doesn't want us to know? Maybe she is just scared that we won't like him. I wouldn't be surprised if she was worried about Mums reaction, and as for me, she could be worried I might go into some weird Dad/big brother mode, pointing at him and telling him never to hurt her? or maybe it's just not that serious between them, so she isn't ready? I don't know, but I wish she would open up and tell me.

I suppose me dating Chloe did come as a bit of a shock but I genuinely thought it would make her happy that her brother was dating her best friend, and I love Chloe so much, I think I always have a little bit, when we were growing up she was always hanging around with Scarlett, and I certainly had a soft spot for her but it was one night in our summer house that really made us both realised just how we felt about each other and Chloe certainly was not shy in telling me!

That had been the start of our relationship, Mum was happy for us but Scarlett and Richard, Chloe's dad didn't seem quite so pleased, everything has just been a bit tough lately, I want everyone to get on, and everyone to be happy, me and Chloe are planning to leave soon, move away and have a fresh start, one day get married hopefully and maybe even have children.

I really wish I could get on better with Richard, he doesn't seem to like me anywhere near as much as he use to when we were all little, I suppose it is a dads job to disapprove of their daughters boyfriends, and uphold the impression that they are scary and not someone to be messed with, especially if that person ever hurt their daughter but he just doesn't seem to want to get to know me at all, or even give me a chance, which I just don't understand at all, surely by now he knows that I am not going anywhere so is it not time to try and improve our relationship with each other, for Chloe's sake if no one else's.

He also seems to have stopped wanting to talk to my mum as much as well, and I know they all use to be really good friends when Dad and Elizabeth were still alive, I'm a bit like Chloe, I just cannot understand what we have done that is so wrong, Mum seems to not be sure why Richard is being funny with her as well, maybe he has some personal issues he needs to deal with, but I'm not giving up, I will just try and keep on his good side as much as I can, and will avoid seeing him as much as possible, just to keep out of his way. But it doesn't matter what he does or says, as I won't ever stop loving Chloe, we are going to be together forever so he just needs to start getting use to that fact, as we don't want to leave under a cloud with everyone hating each other, but we will be leaving whatever happens, whether he likes it or not, so surely he wants to salvage his relationship with his daughter. We will just have to see how things play out over the next few days and weeks.

Chapter Seven

Scarlett couldn't believe what was happening, had she actually heard what she thought she had? Chloe and Sam had turned up at their house one afternoon and had told Scarlett and Marie to sit down, telling them they had something to tell them, it had felt a bit serious and Scarlett had been quite worried.

They told them both, that they wanted to move away from Peterborough and have a fresh start away from all the pain and drama they faced by staying here, they said they wanted to get married one day and maybe even start a family and they didn't want to do that here, not anymore.

Marie had been so happy for them, or she certainly looked and sounded like she was anyway, it was sickening, she was telling them she was so happy for them and wanted them to have the best life possible and kept hugging them both, but Scarlett had been in total shock, what about her? What about her and Chloe? How was this the first time she was hearing about this, how could neither Sam or Chloe not have mentioned any of this to her before, they must have known how much this would upset and hurt her, she felt like her Chloe Bubble had just burst and she had to try really hard not to cry in front of Chloe, she didn't know what else to say, she just wanted to run away and cry. They both seemed quite happy to abandon her, Sam knew what life was like for Scarlett with Marie and he was seriously happy to leave her here with HER, she felt angry, Chloe was supposed to love her, you don't leave people behind that you love, this must have been Sam's idea, maybe he was finally fed up with Richard or having to sort of the fights with mum, but they couldn't leave, they just couldn't, she couldn't survive without them.

She had taken Chloe outside to talk to her, she was so upset and angry and she wanted to know what the hell was going on, had Chloe not even thought about her at all, after everything that had happened between them? She lit a cigarette to try and help her calm down, she forgot that Chloe didn't know that she smoked "Scarlett, what are you doing smoking?" Chloe sounded disappointed in her.

Oh Crap she thought "Sorry Chloe, I just do it sometimes to help calm me down, and right now I'm extremely upset so leave it ok"

"I'm sorry, I really am but I want to start a family with Sam, I love him"

"I thought you loved me too"

"I do, I really do, but it's just not the same, I want to get married and have children the proper way Scarlett, and I can't do that with you"

"What are you talking about, same sex couples can get married and have children just like anyone else, that just sounds like an excuse to me"

"I don't mean it like that, I mean that people don't even know we are together, we are having an affair behind Sam's back, we can't stay like this forever can we"

"Why not? It's been working so far"

"Yes well, I want more and I want it with Sam, I never wanted to be a lesbian Scarlett, what we have is different but it's not what I want for my future, I will always love you but I can't stay here anymore and I can't be with you anymore, I need to be loyal to Sam from now on, we should never have done this to him in the first place, as fun as it has been, I just don't want to do it anymore"

"Is there nothing at all, that I can do or say to make you change your mind?"

"I'm Sorry Scarlett, but it's happening whether you like it or not, but it would be easier if we had your support"

"My support? You are breaking my heart right now Chloe, do you not understand that, so no I can't give you my support, can you just go please, I don't want to be anywhere near you right now"

Chloe had looked so sad as she turned and walked back into the house to get Sam, they made their excuses and left

Scarlett felt completely broken, and she just wanted to scream and shout, but she didn't want her mum to know anything was wrong, so she tried to hold it all in, she thought that everything was going ok between her and Chloe, so why couldn't they just stay and then nothing had to change? Chloe seemed so adamant that this was the only option but why was she being so quick to leave Scarlett behind? They were planning a future that Scarlett wanted, this was Scarlett's Dream and she was not going to let anyone stop her from getting what she wanted with Chloe, She knew she had at least one ally on her side that might be able to help her stop them, as she knew Chloe's Dad Richard was not very happy about their relationship, he was very protective of Chloe and there had been several altercations between Richard and Sam over the years – clearly that hadn't been enough to push Sam away up to now but tensions were high between them. She decided she would go and see Richard, to see if he could help stop them going, but she needed to think of something else that might work too just in case he wasn't interested in helping but also she knew it was likely that no matter what he did or said, Chloe and Sam would still go, he couldn't really stop them, they had made their minds up and were both very stubborn.

Sam could NOT take Chloe away from her, especially now she knew everything she did after reading Marie's diary, there was no way she was going to let him do it, she knew she needed to stop him. There was no time to waste, everything was going terribly wrong and very fast! She needed to come up with a plan and quickly, she felt herself panicking, that wasn't going to help, she needed to sort herself out and regain control.

She knew that the only real way she could stop them going, was if something happened to Sam, so she would have to get Sam completely out of the picture somehow before there was ever going to be a chance of convincing Chloe to be with her again and not Sam. Chloe and Sam seemed to be so in love with each other, it was sickening at times, how on earth would she be able to split them up? She knew this was not going to be easy at all and she really didn't want to hurt Chloe, even if she had just hurt her.

Scarlett knew that she would have to wait for things to settle down after whatever she decided to do about Sam and that she would have to make sure she was there for Chloe, she would look after her, love her and let her know she could rely and depend on her no matter what and soon Chloe would come to her senses she hoped and realise that Scarlett was the only one that was always there for her and always had been, and then they could eventually be together properly and Scarlett could NOT wait for that day! It was going to be a very rough ride for everyone involved but the prize at the end was going to be 100% worth it, Chloe was the girl of her dreams, she always had been and always would be and Scarlett was prepared to do WHATEVER it took to achieve that dream, no one was going to stop her or get in her way.

Chapter Eight

Scarlett had thought a lot about what would really be the best thing to do, in order for her plan to work. She had been planning for a while now and had finally come to a decision about what the first part of her plan was going to be and she was ready to put it into action.

She had decided that she was going to try and make Richard angry and to do this, she knew if she could get to him first, before Chloe or even Sam, and tell him about Chloe and Sam wanting to move away that it would be a pretty good start. She knew that he would not only hate that they were planning to move away, but he would also hate finding out from someone else before Chloe could tell him, she just hoped he didn't direct that anger at her, for being the one to give him the bad news he did have quite a temper and was very protective of Chloe, he would definitely not be happy about any of this, she couldn't help smiling to herself though as she was finally putting her plan into action.

Scarlett found herself pulling up outside Richard and Chloe's house, she was feeling some very mixed emotions, this was the first step of her plan and it felt very important to her, but she also knew that Richard had a temper which made her a tiny bit nervous, she knew that she needed to be extremely careful not to make him too angry in case he lashed out and hurt her that was definitely NOT part of her plan. She knew that she had to pull this off no matter what, so there was simply no stopping her now, she knocked loudly on the front door, she wanted to make sure he heard the door and she knew Chloe wasn't there.

Richard opened the door, unsure who was the other side, as he wasn't expecting anyone.

"Oh, Hi Scarlett what are you doing here? Chloe isn't here I'm afraid, she has already left for work"

"I know, I've just spoken to her, it was you I wanted to speak to actually, is it alright for me come in?"

"Yes of course" he opened the door further to give her enough room to get in, she had known Richard and Chloe for a long time, their families had all been friends and she would see him in the pub where she worked sometimes, obviously he was a lot older than her but they did actually get on quite well most of the time, and this helped as it meant it wasn't too weird to be here without Chloe.

Thankfully she had been to Chloe's house so many times that she knew exactly where everything was, she would need to find an excuse to go upstairs as she needed to get Richards DNA sample so she could prove he was Sam's dad. She knew she would need to be quick so decided to try and get the DNA sample first, then she could tell him about Chloe and Sam's plans second, then she could get out of there quickly if she needed to.

She didn't waste any time and told him she had something to tell him, but first she needed the toilet, he said he would put the kettle on, and went into the kitchen, she ran upstairs, where the only toilet in the house was, and went straight into the bathroom, she grabbed Richards comb that was in a pot near the sink and she put it in a plastic bag that she already had in her pocket, making sure it didn't touch anything else, she flushed the toilet and ran the tap so that Richard wouldn't suspect anything and with the comb safely hidden inside her jacket she reappeared, without Richard suspecting a thing.

"So, what is it you needed to tell me?" Richard asked as he saw her coming into the kitchen, and he signalled for her to sit down as he came to join her with the tea he had just made

"Did you know that Chloe and Sam are planning to move away? She said "They apparently want to get married and start a family away from here" she scoffed as if it was such a ludicrous idea.

"What, no I didn't know that, what are they thinking?" he sounded like he was already getting a bit wound up, Scarlett's plan was working faster than she had anticipated. Up to now she had always wondered why he was so against them being together, but now she knew what she did, it all made sense.

"I never wanted them to be together in the first place, I'm not letting him take my daughter away from me, I've let this go on for far too long now"

"Why are you so against them, I know I'm not Sam's biggest fan all the time, but you REALLY don't like him do you?

She knew from her mums diaries that he knew exactly who Sam was so he was playing a very dangerous game and she wondered what his answer would be, he got up and started pacing around the room.

"It's complicated, really complicated Scarlett and something that I vowed never to tell anyone because of the damage it could cause, but this feels like it is starting to get out of hand and I need to do something to stop it, this wasn't supposed to happen, none of it, why did she let it happen? she said she would sort it all out, I just don't know what to do anymore" he sat down on the bottom step of the stairs and hung his head in his hands

"Who are you talking about?" Scarlett probed, he must be talking about Mum she thought

He looked up at her "I told you, I vowed to never tell anyone, this has got nothing to do with you Scarlett, you need to go, you shouldn't be here" he got up and he ushered her out the door and slammed it shut behind her. He had no idea what she knew.

"Well that went well" she said to herself " he's pretty angry now, maybe even a bit worried, will he try and ring my mum? Will he try and stop them going? and if so how? let's see what he does next, he is bound to want to talk to them, I know Sam acts like he is not bothered by Richard, but I know deep down he is scared of him, he is not a man you want to get on the wrong side of, he was so protective of Chloe I think he would do ANYTHING to stop her leaving, a bit like me I guess, we have the same goal, to STOP CHLOE LEAVING!!

No one will ever suspect I had anything to do with as long as Richard can keep his cool and act like he doesn't already know when Chloe tells him, but she did think that was fairly unlikely as he was pretty annoyed. Chloe and Sam might wonder how he would already know, if they suspected her in any way, then she would have to come up with something to say to make her seem innocent. Her plan was to wind Richard up enough so that he would then do something to Sam, and she just hoped the plan didn't back fire and that he wouldn't do or say anything to Chloe to upset or hurt her, she questioned whether this had really been a good idea but it was too late now, unless she warned Chloe but then she would know that she had spoken to Richard, she just had to wait and see how this played out.

Chapter Nine

Chloe was woken up with a start as her alarm went off for the 3rd time she had overslept and as she looked over at the clock, she realised how late she was for work, damn it she thought, why did I snooze my alarm twice, she was annoyed with herself as she hated being late, and was hardly ever late, it wasn't in her nature.

The bright winter sun was starting to peek through the curtains, and the radiator was starting to rumble as the heating came on. She went to get herself out of bed and realised she couldn't put any weight on her left wrist, she touched it and felt the pain shoot through her body, it must be broken she thought to herself, "great, not! I'm going to have mess about going to the hospital now and get it checked out, I have a headache as well so I probably should get checked for concussion, this really is not what I need right now" she was so annoyed

"I can't believe I fell down the stairs, but then I guess that's what happens when you have an argument with your dad right at the top of them. Sam was only supposed to be dropping me off home, and I was originally going to tell my dad about our plans on my own but then I decided at the last minute that it would be better for us to do it together, I think I wanted and needed Sam there as support as I knew my Dad wouldn't be very happy, but it all kicked off spectacularly, I was not expecting that reaction at all.

"We walked through the front door and Dad was already standing waiting for us, we told him we had something to tell him and he just told Sam that he was not talking his daughter ANYWHERE! and from there things just went from bad to worse, did he know about our plan already or was it just a lucky guess? Either way, he wasn't happy, and neither was Sam and they just started arguing and shouting at each other, throwing insults around and then dad punched Sam right in the mouth, I couldn't believe it, I shouted at him to stop and told Sam he needed to go and that I would speak to him tomorrow, I was so angry at my dad and I couldn't believe how things had escalated.

When Sam had gone, dad stormed off up the stairs and I followed him, I was trying to ask him what on earth was going on, why had he just hit Sam like that? It wasn't like him at all, he may have had a few minor altercations with Sam since we had started dating, but never anything like this, I had never seen him hit someone before, and I really didn't like it and certainly didn't like seeing them arguing like that.

Why could he not just be happy for us, he was starting to behave like Scarlett. He seemed to be so against us being together, they both claimed to love me and care about me so why didn't they want me to be happy? what have either of us done that was SO wrong that no one we love and care about apart from Marie, seem to want us to be together or happy. Why can't they see how much I love Sam, this wasn't just some random boy I had brought home one day, we have known each other our whole lives and we have been through so much together, we were meant to be"

Everyone use to get on so well, Sam and Scarlett's parents, Marie and Matthew had been really good friends with Chloe's Parents Elizabeth and Richard when they were little and they only lived a few doors down from each other, They had shared some great times together, either as families together or just the children playing together but once Elizabeth and Matthew had both died everyone started to slowly drift apart, it was like no one could cope being around each anymore, but the children had all stayed friends and the bonds they shared became stronger because of what they had all been through at such a young age and not many other children could relate.

She knew her dad was over protective of her, most dads are protective of their daughters, it kicks in as soon as you are born, but it had got worse when Elizabeth had committed suicide and ever since then he has wanted to know what is going on, where she is, who she is with almost every minute of the day, but this felt different this time, he was angry but seemed upset too and he almost looked shocked when he hit Sam, maybe he had realised it all got a bit too much now, but when she tried to talk to him at the top of the stairs, they had continued to argue, Chloe had said she couldn't listen to this anymore and went to turn and go back downstairs, but she had slipped and fell all the way to the bottom, she got up saying she was fine and ran out the front door to calm down, she didn't want to be anywhere near her dad at that moment, and she waited till she thought he would be in bed, before she went home, she just couldn't face him.

She got her dad to drop her off at the hospital, she had convinced him she was ok last night but just wanted to be left alone after having their argument but now she really needed to get checked out, she rang Sam and told him what had happened, he didn't believe her when she said it was just an accident and was angry, Sam and Richard did not really get on very well sadly which was really hard as she loved them both, she asked Sam to meet her at the hospital but had no idea if he actually would as when he said he would, he didn't really sound like he was paying attention to her, and she was worried that he might try and go to see her dad but knew he would not like being accused of hurting her, not after everything that happened with her mum and she really didn't want things to get any worse between them.

Richard had asked Chloe if she wanted him to stay with her at the hospital but she said she would be fine on her own, even though she still felt upset she told him she loved him and they both apologised for arguing with each other the night before, they hugged each other and that's all she wanted in that moment, but she was still going to move away with Sam, whether her dad or Scarlett liked it or not! So sadly she knew this wasn't going to be the end of the conversation and she really wanted her dad to apologise to Sam too as what he did was totally uncalled for, he said he would think about it, but she didn't hold out much hope, I guess at least he was considering it which was a start sort of.

Chloe could not help thinking back to the moment she realised she was in love with Sam, it had been a rollercoaster of emotions the last few years but it had all been worth it to be with him.It had been summer, Marie had a summer house in the bottom of the garden and it was the children's den, on this occasion Scarlett was staying with her grandparents and Sam was having a little get together with some friends, and had invited Chloe along too. She could still remember just how magical that summer house felt when you were inside, there were fairy lights everywhere and fluffy blankets and cushions, by the end of the night there was just 4 of them left, the other 2 looked like they might have been in a relationship so it felt a bit like they were on a double date. Chloe had fancied Sam for quite a while by this point but had not done anything about it, but then Sam picked up his guitar and started singing and it just felt like he was signing directly to her, it was like there was no one else in the room, they couldn't take their eyes of each other, it was amazing and she realised she was in love with him, right there and then and she needed to let him know.

The 2 other friends left and Sam was getting ready to walk Chloe home, he was leaning against the wall of the house waiting for Chloe to get her stuff, and she stood in front of him and just said "I really like you, you know" and then just lent in straight away and kissed him, and before she had time to feel embarrassed about what she had done, he was kissing her back! She couldn't believe it, it was the best moment ever!

They ended up upstairs in Sam's room and she could still remember how electric his touch felt as he undressed her slowly, never taking his eyes off her, she was in heaven and felt happier than she had ever felt before, she loved him so much! They had agreed that it might not be a good idea to still be there in the morning because of his mum and scarlett so after they had made love and got themselves sorted out, he walked her home, giving her another kiss before she went in and shut the door, she had stood the other side of the door, leant her head back and slid down to the floor, closing her eyes, remembering what had just happened, she had a massive smile on her face and it was like a dream come true.

That had been the start of their incredible relationship and she couldn't get enough of him, in the back of her mind she always feared he would find someone else and leave her but he never did, and when he said he wanted to move away with her, get married and start a family it was music to her ears, so nothing and no one was going to stop her and Sam from doing what they both wanted to do.

She had no idea if Sam was still friends with anyone from that night, she certainly couldn't remember any of their names, it had all been about Sam that night and nobody else! She felt a tinge of guilt as she now recalled this memory after everything that has happened with Scarlett since that night, thankfully Scarlett never quite knew all the facts about how they got together as she had a feeling she wouldn't have been very happy about it, life felt a bit messy at the minute and she would need to try and sort things out with her dad and speak to Scarlett too. Moving away couldn't come soon enough, she was ready for this new chapter in her life.

Chapter Ten

Richard felt himself starting to get a bit reflective on his life recently, he didn't think he was the type of person to sit and reflect but so much had happened that he felt he needed to try and process it all somehow. It felt like a total and utter mess now and neither him or Marie knew what to do to even begin starting to sort any of it out.

He sometimes wished he had never met Marie, and never starting having an affair with her, because if he hadn't done any of that, then none of the things that they were facing now would ever have happened but he also felt guilty for feeling like that, as he had loved Marie when they were together and he had been a completely willing participant in the affair, he certainly hadn't needed his arm twisting very much, they had just hit it off with each other right from the first time they met, and never thought that they would end up having an affair but she was so sad and lonely because Matthew was never there, he was always working away and she was just seeking some comfort and she couldn't get that from Elizabeth even though they were best friends and he didn't know why but he had just let himself succumb to the temptations and soon they were having an passionate affair and their feelings for each other were developing more and more, but he never stopped loving Elizabeth, he loved her SO much more, it was just different with Elizabeth, she was his wife, they had made a commitment to each other and they were trying for a baby, he knew what he was doing was wrong and not fair at all on Elizabeth or Matthew but he just couldn't stop himself.

Elizabeth was his whole life and he loved her more than anything else, and he felt so guilty for loving Marie as well because she was not worth losing Elizabeth for, but Marie was more fun than Elizabeth and life had become all about trying for a baby and it had sort of taken the joy out of things and he had been worried that a baby might change things for the worse, so it had been exciting for him to have Marie in his life, sneaking around and no one knowing what they were doing, the sex was just fun too, not scheduled and only to make a baby like with Elizabeth but there was never going to come a time when he would leave Elizabeth for her, no matter what she might have thought or hoped, he had never wanted to hurt Marie, but they were having an affair, they were not in a proper relationship, so what did she expect, most men don't leave their wives and deep down she knew that, that's why she never left Matthew.

He didn't know how long things would continue between them and often wondered if he should end things before it got any worse, knowing he was never going to leave Elizabeth to be with Marie, how long was too long when you knew it wouldn't end the way you wanted it to, but then Marie told him she was pregnant and suddenly everything changed between them and there was simply no going back after that. Richard felt guilt like he had never felt before because he and Elizabeth had been trying for a baby for so long, and now he had got Marie pregnant and not Elizabeth, he had failed his wife so much, it was the worst kind of betrayal, he had let Elizabeth down massively and he needed to fix it somehow and fast, she didn't deserve ANY of this.

Marie had foolishly wanted them to be a family, but that was never going to be an option, it was just a fantasy as Richard just couldn't do that to Elizabeth and so he told her that he would do his best to look after her and the baby but it would have to be discreetly and that the affair would have to end straight away. He wanted to own up and tell the truth so many times but he knew how devasted Elizabeth would be, so he tried to carry on like everything was ok, but inside he felt utter shame for what he had done.

Things had started to dwindle between them quite quickly after that, but they realised they still couldn't be a part and so they didn't stop seeing each other, they carried on, on and off, while she was pregnant and they even tried to carry things on, once Sam was born and Matthew was working away a lot again, but for Richard it felt like It wasn't really working anymore, it didn't feel right, he couldn't give Marie what she wanted, and all he was doing was dragging out the inevitable because once Elizabeth got pregnant that would be it for him and the affair would end, but it all went wrong and he could still remember the day vividly and every single day of his life, he wished that he could go back in time and change everything he missed his wife so much and hated himself for causing Chloe to grow up without her mum, who had loved her so, so much, he wished every single day that he could take Elizabeth's place and give Chloe her mum back.

Elizabeth and Richard had been blessed with a baby a couple of years later, and it was when Chloe was 6, Marie had gone on to have Scarlett with Matthew and she was also now 6, they were going round for a play date for the 1st time, but the second Sam had walked into the living room Elizabeth just froze and she could not take her eyes of him, Richard could tell by her face that she just knew that Sam was HIS son, He didn't know how she knew but she just did! Did Sam really look that much like him? He must have done. Elizabeth didn't say or do anything until everyone had left, the whole play date had been unbearable and then once everyone had gone, they had a massive row which thankfully Chloe didn't hear, or at least that's what they both hoped, as Richard went on to confess everything to Elizabeth and he had begged for her forgiveness but a month later she was dead, and it was all his fault, she couldn't bear the thought of what he and Marie had done, or that they had a child together and she just couldn't cope anymore, she was hurting so much, her life had been destroyed and Marie and Richard were the reason she decided to kill herself, to end her life and leave her little girl without a mummy, the guilt was still too much to bear, Richard felt that he had caused an unbelievable amount of pain and his poor little girl was the one that had suffered the most, losing her mummy at just 6 years old, life was never the same after that for any of them.

"I should never have let Sam and Chloe be friends as they started growing up, let alone, leave them to get together into a relationship but I just didn't know how to stop it, if I had told them what the reason was then it would have been catastrophic for not only their relationship but mine and Chloe's too and I just couldn't take that risk, I couldn't bear to lose her. I have become so angry and even more over protective as Chloe has got older and I think I am slowly starting to push her away, and that's really not what I want to do at all, I love her so, so much and I feel like I have already lost so much, I can't lose Chloe too.

Now Scarlett is interfering and telling me that Chloe and Sam are planning to move away, what is she playing at, she must know that is something that Chloe would want to tell me first, it's not her place to tell me, stupid girl. I barely ever speak to Marie anymore, it is just way too awkward, I do wonder how she is feeling about all this though, Chloe said she was happy for them, but how can she be. She must be pretending so she doesn't give anything away. I need to stop it, I just don't know how and I can't believe I hit Sam tonight... I hit my own Son in the face, how could I do that? I was so angry and upset, I just saw red, he wants to take Chloe away from me, my baby girl and I simply can't let him do that, ever. We started arguing, both throwing insults at each other and I lost it with him, I have never, ever wanted to hurt him but it is just so bloody difficult for me, I can't treat him like my son because that would seem a bit strange, and especially now he is dating Chloe, that would be even stranger, I have had to just act like any normal dad would, simply protecting their daughter but I wish I had a better relationship with Sam especially since Matthew is no longer with us either, we have all been through so much and Sam needed a dad just as much as Chloe needed a mum, it's such an awful situation, I've not done right by Sam at all and it's not his fault.

I also caused Chloe to fall down the stairs tonight when we were having a stupid argument, it was a complete accident, she just turned at the top of the stairs and missed the step and fell down, but if I had not been in the foul mood I was, if I had not hit Sam in the face then we wouldn't have been arguing in the first place, I just don't seem to be able to get anything right, ever and now I have hurt Chloe too, she took quite a fall but said she was ok, I wanted to check on her properly but she stormed out of the house slamming the front door behind her, so I knew she needed some space and time to calm down, I just hoped and prayed that she was ok and that she would be back before I woke up the next morning. I'm not happy with Scarlett though, she caused all this with her stirring, she knows what

I'm like, surely she knew this would wind me up so why would she tell me before Chloe could, what does she get out of this, what does she have to gain? I don't trust her, she has change since was little, so much more than Sam and Chloe have, I think she is a bit of a trouble maker, rebelling and she must be a handful for Marie especially as a single parent.

Chapter Eleven

Scarlett had always liked watching things like crime dramas, thriller and horror films and even true stories about prolific killers, she was so fascinated by it all and often wished she had gone to university to study psychology or criminology so she could understand it all better, but of course instead she had stayed, not wanting to leave Chloe, who didn't want to go to university because of Sam, but lately she had started to have very vivid dreams about death, killing, torture – real dark stuff and they were becoming more realistic and she found herself starting to research well known death and murder cases online, but she couldn't quite work out why she was suddenly so much more interested than before or why on earth she was dreaming about it so much. None of this felt normal, it wasn't like she was planning to kill anyone, she could never do that, or could she… she paused for a moment, maybe this wasn't just a coincidence, was the universe trying to send her a message or some sort of sign? She couldn't help wondering if this could be a genuine option.

Could killing Sam be the answer? no it couldn't be, she wasn't a killer, killers were horrible evil psychopaths, that wasn't her but it suddenly dawned on her that thought of killing actually, excited her. She couldn't believe it and was very surprised at how she felt as this wasn't what she thought she wanted at all and she didn't think she was capable of it either, but the thought had definitely now sparked something inside her but what now? She decided she needed to sleep on it, none of this felt real she need clear head to process it all fully. When she woke up the next morning she still felt the same, and the thought only got stronger as the days went by until finally she had decided she was doing it and she wasn't going to waste any time, it was happening, today was going to be the day, maybe so she didn't talk herself out of it, it's not every day you wake up and decide to kill your own brother.

This really was the last resort so she wanted to give Sam one final chance, maybe if she told him what she knew then he would realise for himself that the best thing to do would be to end things with Chloe and leave for good, but Scarlett knew how stubborn he was, so she just had to see how things went, but one way or another, Sam was going to be out of Chloe's life for good by the end of the day, her patience had run out.

Scarlett knew that their mum would be out for the night till late, which gave her till at least 10pm she thought. It needed to be done at night so that if she had to go ahead and kill him, hopefully no one would see or suspect anything.

It had finally come down to this, enough was enough, there was no backing out now, it had to be now or never, she didn't really know how she was going to do it, but what she did know was this would all be over soon! So as Sam went off to work, Scarlett stayed in her room and spent the day planning what to do if she killed Sam, how would she dispose of his body, clean up etc although she couldn't quite bring herself to think about the main part properly, as the thought of actually committing that final cruel act was just a little too much for her to bare, she was killing her own brother after all, her own flesh and blood, the only one that looked after her and loved her when she was little, unlike her waste of space mother but she had to try and focus on the end goal, and shut out any feelings she might still have for Sam.

She patiently sat in the kitchen, waiting for Sam to come home from work, Marie had already gone out so Scarlett had cooked them both dinner and was watching TV just as Sam walked in, she hadn't actually seen him since last night when he had his fight with Richard

"What happened to you" she asked hinting at his face, she already knew what had happened of course, after a phone call with Chloe but she wanted to see what he would tell her

"Oh, I had a little falling out with Richard, I don't really want to talk about it, though, ok"

"Oh come on Sam, what really happened as it looks like more than just a little falling out, have you actually seen your face?" she got her phone out and took a picture of him and turned the phone round to show him "Also, Chloe has ended up in hospital with a broken wrist and concussion so what the hell happened"

Sam signed, he knew Scarlett was right, but he just felt so fed up of the battle he and Chloe seemed to face every day just to be together, it was really starting to get to both of them now and they just wanted things to stop

"I dropped Chloe off as normal last night, she decided she wanted us to tell Richard together, about us moving away as she couldn't wait any longer, but it was strange because as we walked in the house and he was already stood there waiting for us and he seemed angry! we got into an argument, we both said some pretty unpleasant things to each other and then he punched me! Chloe shouted at him and then told me to leave, I didn't want to leave her behind but thought it was best to get out of there quick in case I made things worse. I'm so sick of it Scarlett, we need to get out of here and as soon as we can, and I'm pretty sure he pushed her down the stairs, she keeps saying it was an accident but I don't believe her, I saw how angry he was when I left, I just never assumed he would ever hurt her otherwise I would never have left"

"Do you really think it's a good idea to leave though Sam, you've seen what he is capable of, do you honestly think he will let you take Chloe away from him?"

"Yes I do think it's a good idea Scarlett, because what is keeping us here? it's not like we want to move to the other side of the world is it, we just want a bit of distance between us and Richard and maybe the distance will make him see what he is at risk of losing"

"You don't seem to have learnt anything though Sam, you are not meant to be together why can you not see that?" Scarlett wanted to know why he wouldn't just give in and move on

"Why shouldn't we be together? just because Richard doesn't like me, that is not going to stop us Scarlett, is hasn't up to now, and it never will"

"No that's not what I meant"

"Then why, Scarlett, go on tell me please, because I would REALLY like to know why my own sister and my girlfriends dad cannot just be happy for us!"

"Because...." she paused, could she really tell him the truth? of course she could, here was her moment to bring his world down around him and she did sort of hope that he would just give up and leave, that maybe she would spare his life, even though she knew deep down that he would never give up that easily.

"Because you are related Sam that's why!" she shouted at him "Richard is your dad!"

"What a load of rubbish, why on earth would you say such a stupid thing are you really that twisted that you would make up such a horrible thing like that, what is wrong with you, you are so bitter and twisted Scarlett, I know life has been tough and I have no explanation as to why mum is the way she is with you but I have always looked after you and loved you, so why would you do this to me and Chloe?" he looked so upset

"I thought you would react like this, so I have proof! she tried to show him the pictures in her phone that she had taken of her mums diary "Mum has got a diary, its ALL in there Sam look I took pictures of the pages" but as she tried to

128

show him the phone, he knocked it away he didn't believe her and he wasn't even going to entertain the idea

"I am not interested in whatever fake documents or pictures you have created Scarlett, just get out of my way please" he pushed past her so he could leave the room, he wanted to go and see Chloe even though she was still in hospital and tell her that he wanted to move away as soon as possible, once she was well enough, he was so done with all of this.

"Ok then, what about the DNA test I had done? she said confidently, she was bluffing now as she had not actually had the test done but Sam didn't know that.

He stopped, and turned to face her "More lies Scarlett, why do you keep doing this? why are you being so nasty and vindictive? do you not get enough attention from all of us, is that what it is, or are you enjoying this?"

Scarlett wasn't anxious anymore, she was wound up and the rage was starting to bubble up inside her, why would he not believe her? why couldn't he at least look at the photos, or actually listen to what she was trying to tell him, she wasn't lying, she was so angry, she stamped her foot hard on the kitchen floor "Listen to me Sam" she shouted at him "I am NOT lying, you need to believe me, this is not a joke"

"Whatever Scarlett, I'm not listening to you anymore, I have lost interest, all you and Richard are doing is making me and Chloe realise that what we are planning to do is completely the right thing, we need to get away from ALL of you and I'm going to go and tell Chloe right now that we need to leave sooner rather than later"

Scarlett could not let him leave, this wasn't over and as he went to walk away from her, it was like the rage had suddenly taken over her body, she saw red and she was no longer in control, before she really knew what she was doing, she had grabbed one of the kitchen knives that was in a stand on the worktop and charged towards him with it in her hand, screaming "you're not going anywhere" Sam stopped and turned to see what all the noise was, she plunged the knife straight into his chest without a second thought, they both looked at each other and then down at the knife, Scarlett could see the fear and confusion in Sam's eyes, she felt a rush of adrenaline, she had enjoyed that a bit too much, maybe she was evil after all, and she had just let out her inner monster. She knew this would help her get exactly what she had always wanted so it was all worth it, no matter what the cost was to anyone else why hadn't she thought of this sooner.

Scarlett looked at him directly into his eyes, and she slowly starting to pull the knife out, Sam tried to stop her but he couldn't and she just stood there and watched as he fell to the floor, he started to cough and was struggling to speak, he landed on the rug in the living room and there was so much blood. Sam tried to reach for his phone but could barely move as the pain seared through his body, he tried to put his hands over the stab wound but the blood just kept coming, what the hell was happening, his own sister had just stabbed him, he couldn't believe it, his life flashed before him, he thought of Chloe and his mum, he couldn't die, he needed help. Scarlett reached into his pocket and took his phone out of his pocket, and as she bent down to get closer to him she slowly rested her head against his, closed her eyes and quietly said to him "I'm so sorry Sam, I really am but this is what you get for not listening to me, I gave you a chance to save yourself and you chose not to take it, this had to happen so that I can be with Chloe. If you had just walked away, then I wouldn't have had to do this, although it does mean I am taking mums precious son away from her which is only the start of the punishment I have planned for her"

Sam tried to put his hands on Scarlett's, but he couldn't move, he felt so helpless and alone, he was devasted at what was happening, because he knew he was dying and Scarlett wasn't doing anything to help him, she had completely lost the plot, why was she talking about Chloe like that? why would he ever have walked away from her, how could he have known what was really going on, this wasn't fair, he was in so much pain and tried to shout for help but no sound was coming from his mouth, and he was struggling to keep his eyes open, he didn't want to die, he didn't want to even think about never see Chloe again, or think about the pain she would be in, knowing it would trigger feelings of losing her mum all over again, and what about Marie, was she safe? if Scarlett was capable of doing this to him, then it wasn't such a crazy thought that she might be planning to do the same to Marie too, but it was too late now, he couldn't do anything to protect them, or help himself, he simply couldn't fight anymore, he felt so weak, he saw Scarlett stand up and throw his phone away from him, so that he couldn't reach it, that's when he realised for certain that she wasn't going to call for help, she wasn't going to try and save him. She never took her eyes off him the whole time and as a tear fell from his cheek and his eyes closed for the final time, she knew he was dead, her hands were shaking as she pulled her sleeve down over them to check his pulse, there was nothing, he was definitely gone, she had killed him.

She fell back against the sofa, and tears suddenly filled her eyes, she couldn't believe what she had just done, she knew this was what she had planned but she had never killed someone before, and until yesterday, never thought she would ever kill someone, but now her brother was lying in front of her dead, she had never seen a dead body this close before and it was not a pleasant sight, the tears came harder and faster and she felt confused because she didn't expect to feel this way, Sam being dead meant she got everything she had ever wanted but in that moment she realised just how much she loved Sam and that's why it hurt so much.

She knew her mum wouldn't be back for quite a while but she also couldn't sit there all night in case Marie came home early, so she sat there just watching his lifeless body lying there, for a while, she couldn't take her eyes of him it was like she was in a trance, but she slowly started to come round and realised she needed to get this all cleared up, but how? ring an ambulance or the police? They wouldn't think this was an accident, or that she just found him like this, how could she explain what had happened, no she needed to hide the body, just until she could work out what to do next.

She needed to hide his body somewhere, but it couldn't be anywhere in the house. She needed to get him outside and into her car. She had fairly good upper body strength so was able to wrap him in the rug and pull him through the house and into the garden, thankfully she had parked her car round the back and the gates were shut so no one could see what was going on, with all her might she heaved his body into the boot of her car and slammed the boot shut, she went back inside the house and cleaned up the mess in the house thanking her lucky stars that Marie had vinyl everywhere so it was easy to clean, she didn't really know what to do next but she knew she couldn't stay at home so got in her car and just started to drive.

She had not been driving for very long when she realised that she was near the woods, that she had driven past so many times in her life, she headed in as far as she could with the car and stopped, she took a deep breath, she couldn't quite believe that she had her brothers body in the boot of her car, her dead brother! She decided she had no other choice but to bury him, she was so nervous about burying him, his was like something out of a horror film, like the ones she had been watching, she needed to make sure he was never found, or if he was that she was never caught and luckily she still had some gardening tools in the car after borrowing them from a neighbour to help tidy up the garden, she realised this meant that she could bury Sam today and get this over and done with and be home for dinner, not that she wanted dinner with Marie.

It was pretty dark now, and it was also very cold and eery in the woods, she kept telling herself she wasn't scared and it made her remember the ghost stories her grandad would tell her when she was younger, she would always pretend and say to him that she wasn't scared and would tell him not to stop "more Grandad, more" she would say laughing but inside she was petrified and he always knew just how to make her jump, but it made her laugh every time and it was just something they did together with no one else which she really liked, she loved her grandad so much although she couldn't help thinking just how disappointed he would be with her now if he knew what she had done, she always wished he wasn't getting older and that he was just normal grandad again but at least with his condition, he would never know about any of this, she felt extremely sad and guilty to think what her grandad would think of her if he did know, she knew she had let him down and he would be so disappointed in her.

Collecting her thoughts, she kept reminding herself why she was doing all this, her beautiful Chloe who would soon be falling into her arms after losing everyone else she loved, and she would finally realise that it was Scarlett she needed and no one else. It had actually been Chloe that had helped her to form this plan how ironic, lots of scenarios had been through Scarlett's mind since they started their affair and she knew she wanted Chloe all to herself sooner rather than later, she had started to think about all the different ways she could get rid of Sam permanently and if it was going to be death then she needed a scape goat in case his body was ever found. When she had heard that Chloe wanted to move away with Sam, and then she received that call from Chloe telling her that she had fallen down the stairs and hurt herself after having an argument with her dad, Scarlett hadn't believed that she was telling her the truth, even though Chloe had tried to convince her otherwise but she 100% believed that Richard had done it, and NO ONE was going to get away with hurting Chloe, not even her Dad and that's when her plan had started to formulate to get rid of Richard at the same time, she wasn't sure what she was going to do but decided to get some of Richards DNA just in case she decided to do a test and prove to Sam that she was telling the truth, and after that, Scarlett spent ages trying to think of exactly what she could do to get rid of them, both at the same time, she knew Sam wouldn't believe her about the DNA and that she would probably have to kill him and that's when she had suddenly had the idea that the hair she got when she went to see Richard the last time she saw him, could be used for something much better, no longer would it be for the DNA test she had planned to do, it was going to play a bigger part in her plan, she was going to plant Richards hair on Sam's body as evidence instead.

Now the day was here, it was done and all she had to do was somehow get Sam's body out of her car, dig a hole big enough, plant the evidence and bury him all without anyone seeing her, thankfully it was very late now and no one really came into these woods very often, certainly not this late at night but she knew she needed to be quick and not leave anything behind that could trace back to her, this was it, the final stage and it was almost over.

Chapter Twelve

Scarlett had tried as hard as she possible could to bury Sam's body but it had been so tiring digging into the ground to make a hole big enough and it had taken what felt like forever, what make her she think this had been a good idea? she had no other idea though so what else was she going to do with the body if she didn't bury it? She was near the railway track and did briefly think about leaving Sam's body on the track but she knew that was a really bad idea as that would cause several more casualties if there were passengers on the train and that didn't seem fair plus it would definitely cause there to be an investigation and the place would get covered with police, so she knew that wouldn't work, she needed to make sure that

Sam would never get found, and that no one would even consider that he might be buried in the woods, but she did also want to make sure that Richard would be the prime suspect when no one could find him, or his body or worst case if he ever was found, she wanted to make sure it was Richard who went down for the murder and not her! She was making sure all bases were covered, she was finally going to be with Chloe properly and forever this time, so she had to make sure that she could never get caught.

She knew that once the police knew Sam was missing that she could tell them she knew about the fight Sam and Richard had not long before Sam went missing, which was true as Richard had a bit of a falling out with Sam when they tried to discuss what Sam and Chloe had planned, Sam had come home with a split lip and a bruised face and Chloe had seen it all, her dad just went mad and hit Sam in the face. Scarlett had managed to get a picture as well just in case she needed proof of what she was saying. It was a waiting game now her as she knew Chloe or Marie would report Sam missing and then people would be looking for him.

She left the woods and headed back to her car having done all she could, Sam was buried and evidence planted just in case anyone ever did find his body. It was dark now and she was freezing cold as she had left her coat at home, it suddenly made her wonder how cold Sam would get buried under the soil and she found herself staring at his make shift grave, taking in what she had done, she expected to feel something guilt or sadness maybe, but no she turned to walk away with a smile on her face, she had taken her mums precious son away from her and she had finally got him out of Chloe's life for good, she only wished she had thought about killing him sooner and was a little frustrated that she wouldn't be able to look her mum in the eyes and tell her exactly what she had done! Years of not being loved enough or even noticed enough had turned Scarlett into a monster but she truly believed she could pretend that none of this had ever happened, comfort Chloe through her pain and eventually get the girl of her dreams all to herself. When she made it back to the car, she got in and felt herself relax but she was surprised that she suddenly felt quite emotional, now she had stopped, it had hit her all at once but she wasn't entirely sure if it was because of Sam or that she knew she was going to be with Chloe soon, she hoped it was a bit of both as she didn't want to be a total psychopath.

It was not long before Scarlett was back home, there were no lights on in the house, so she knew Marie must be in bed. She crept in quietly making sure not to wake her up, and she was soon in her own bed fast asleep completely unaware that the rain was slowly starting to fall outside.

Chapter Thirteen

The next morning as Scarlett began to wake slowly she felt so tired and quickly noticed that her whole body ached a lot, for a split second she questioned why, before it all came flooding back to her, she stared into space momentarily while she thought about everything and how she would have to try and hide that her body ached so much it was painful, because she had to make sure she didn't raise any suspicions, as she couldn't exactly say she had been for a work out as everyone knew she hated exercise.

She got up to open her curtains, her window had been open slightly so the first thing she noticed was the sound and a damp smell, she slowly pulled back the curtains and saw that it was raining really hard, she instantly felt sick with panic, what if the rain is disturbing Sam's grave? How deep had she dug the hole? Did she make sure all of Sam's body was covered fully with soil? She felt her chest tighten and couldn't breathe properly, she sat back on the edge of bed, and tried to calm herself down, it will all be ok she told herself, hardly anyone ever goes into those woods and it's not like I buried him at the side of the road, she felt proud of herself that she had remembered to go as deep into the woods as she could go, this had been a long time coming and she still almost could not believe that she had managed to pull it off, "I did it, I really did it" she said out loud as a big smile crept across her face, she was proud of herself, but it didn't mask the fear she was also feeling about Sam's grave potentially being discovered.

She knew that she needed to act fast, she needed to tie up all loose ends just in case and then for her own piece of mind she might try and take a quick drive that way just to make sure everything was still ok.

She quickly got dressed and headed over to Richards house. She felt pumped up and excited, she simply could not wait to get to Richard's house and tell him that he had to leave, and for good, but she also felt nervous, as it felt like she hadn't really prepared for this, she had hoped she could have a bit more time but mother nature clearly had other ideas.

She knew he wouldn't take the blackmailing lightly but hoped that he would see what there was to lose if he didn't do exactly what she said and she knew her mums diary would prove useful if she needed it.

As Richard answered the door he was surprised to see her "what are you doing here again Scarlett?"

"Well that's a nice greeting isn't it, thanks" and she just walked straight in, pushing past him, she felt fearless

"I actually have something to show you" she said smiling as she got her phone out of her pocket

"Oh yeh, and what's that then?"

In that moment she felt completely in control, the adrenaline was running through her body, this was it, as she showed Richard the photo she had taken of Sam, dead she watched closely and waited for his reaction

He seemed to freeze, staring at the photo not knowing what to make of it, he looked up at Scarlett "Is this some sort of sick joke, what the hell" he looked angry

"No, this is not a joke Richard, this is deadly serious actually, this is Sam's dead body, I killed him last night and I have framed you for his murder in case his body is ever found"

"What are you talking about?" he was a bit nervous of just how calm she seemed

"I have planted your DNA on his body" she couldn't help smirking as she said this, she was extremely proud of herself, knowing that this was ALL her doing and he had NO way out, she had him trapped and she was loving every minute if it.

Whilst she was basking in her joy, she didn't see Richard suddenly launch himself at her at speed and before she knew what was happening, he had her pinned up against the wall with both his hands around her neck, she couldn't help laughing, she was enjoying this "What are you going to do Richard, prove me right, I always knew you had a temper, the police won't think twice about arresting you for Sam's murder, especially if you do something to me"

He was SO angry but also felt very confused, he let Scarlett go and punched the wall next to her before stepping back, he was annoyed that she seemed to have the upper hand, he needed to stay calm and level headed, he couldn't let her know how much she was getting under his skin but how on earth was he going to get out of this, and why the hell had she killed Sam?

"I don't understand, why on earth did you kill Sam, your own brother, your best friends boyfriend…. oh god my poor Chloe, she is going to be devastated, what have you done you psycho!" he could feel the anger rising inside him again but this time he didn't move, he kept his eyes on Scarlett, waiting for her to answer him

"Chloe is better off without him, and she is better off without you too! she snapped back "and that's why, if you don't leave and never come back, I will tip the police off about Sam" she could feel herself getting angry, everyone just needed to go away and leave her and Chloe alone.

"You're Sick, do you know that! you won't get away with this Scarlett, people will be looking for him, and they will wonder where I've gone too"

"Oh don't you worry yourself about that Richard, I've got that all in hand, trust me, people are going to think Sam has just gone away for a little while, except he won't come back of course, will he" she laughed

"You're evil, do you realise what you are saying to me right now, you are admitting to me, quite calmly I might add, that you have killed someone Scarlett, that's not normal"

"Normal, Ha! Nothing about this is normal is it! I know Everything Richard, about my mum, the affair and I also know that Sam was your Son"

"Rubbish, you don't know what you are talking about" fear flooded through him, how the hell did she know that? it also hit him at that moment that it wasn't just Chloe's boyfriend who was dead, it was his son, he wanted to cry so badly but he knew he couldn't show any emotion in front of Scarlett, she wasn't going to get the better of him, but he just could not believe that this was happening, it was a real life nightmare that he couldn't wake up from.

"Oh my mummy dearest kept a diary, multiple diaries actually and she wrote about literally EVERYTHING, so I know all the sordid details of your affair, how you lost interest in her once she was pregnant and how you caused Elizabeth to kill herself"

"Stupid cow, why on earth did she keep a diary for, did she want us to get caught?" He couldn't believe what he was hearing, they had tried so hard to keep all of that from everyone.

"Oh you really are a piece of work aren't you! Turning on my mum now, well done you really are the perfect father figure aren't you!"

"This is not just my fault Scarlett, your mum was an equal participant in all this, I loved her, I just didn't want a child with her, me and Elizabeth were trying to have a baby and we had Chloe, I couldn't do that to her anymore so I had to end things with your mum, but I did my best to still help her out where I could"

"It is all thanks to you that she hates me! I am the child that wasn't yours and I am just a constant reminder of the family she always wanted but never had, and she has taken that out on me since the day I was born, and you are you both the reason that Chloe has had to grow up without a mum! You both needed to be punished and that is why I killed Sam, rather than either of you 2, because I wanted you to see and feel the same pain you have both caused for me and Chloe"

"But he was your brother Scarlett, don't you care at all, not one little bit that he is dead, that you will never see him again, there is no coming back from this, you can't undo what you have done"

"True, he was my brother yes, and growing up, I couldn't have been without him, he was a great brother but in the end, he became a problem, as he was in the way of me and Chloe being together and he was going to take her away from me, so I had to stop him, and this way I get rid of you at the same time" she was cool, calm and collected and was revelling in all this truth telling that was going on.

Richard sat down on the stairs, he felt completely beaten, he didn't know what to do or say, but he realised that Scarlett was right, he WAS the reason Elizabeth was dead, the reason Chloe didn't have a mum, the reason Marie hated Scarlett, all because of how HE had treated her, he was a failure and Chloe WOULD be better off without him, but how could he just walk out and leave without saying goodbye, equally how could he ever look her in the face again, knowing what he now knew about Sam, his heart hurt so much, he knew just how much pain his little girl would be in once all this came out, and he just wanted to be there to comfort her, but if she knew everything, would she want anything to do with him anymore?

He decided he would do what Scarlett asked, without any shouting or fighting, he needed to get out of there and find somewhere to stay so he could come up with a plan to see Chloe and get Scarlett arrested for all of this, this was not the end, he just had to make Scarlett believe that it was and that she had won.

"Ok, I will go. I will leave today and never come back, but how do I know you will stick the end of your deal?"

"Because I will have Chloe, that's what this is all about, as that's all I have EVER wanted, so as long as you keep out of our way, I will keep up my end of the deal, I'm glad you have realised this is the best thing to do Richard, without putting up a fight, wise decision"

"I don't exactly have much choice do I" he walked up the stairs to his bedroom, so that he could pack a few things, Scarlett stayed downstairs, she wasn't going to leave until she knew he had gone for sure.

He came back down and gave her his door keys "Can I at least leave Chloe a note to say goodbye, she is still in hospital, you can't let her come home to an empty house and have no idea where I am or what has happened to me, that's not fair, not when she will soon have Sam to worry about"

She rolled her eyes and huffed "Quickly, just say that you have had to go and you don't want her to look for you, I can fill in the gaps"

She stood by the front door watching him drive off, feeling a sense of massive relief as that had gone better than she expected and soon this could be their new family home, she couldn't wait for that day to come, she knew there was still a lot to come first, she couldn't make Chloe forget about Sam or her dad that easily but in time, she would get everything she had always wanted.

As Scarlett stood there day dreaming about it all, at that same moment a dog walker was walking through the woods, it was a cold, fresh and foggy day, and although he was use to this route he was still being careful not to trip over anything, in the distance he thought he could see something ahead of him on the floor but with the poor visibility he couldn't make anything out so carried on walking, pulling his dogs lead a little to make sure he stayed close but the nearer they got, the man realised it was what looked (but he couldn't be sure) like a badly dug grave.

He stepped back in shock and fell over, the dog started tugging on his lead wanting to break away, so he had to pull him back as he didn't want him getting to close.

It was unusual to see something like this in the woods as hardly anyone ever came here anymore, so there was very rarely anything that got disturbed. He did not want to get any closer in case it was a grave, so he tried to call the police but realised he didn't have any signal being so deep in the woods. He made his way back to the main road as quickly as he could, with his dog in tow and made the call. He was advised to wait where he was and someone would be with him shortly, when the Police arrived they asked him to show them where he had seen the disturbed area but as it was still so foggy he couldn't remember exactly where he had walked, so they said they would have to wait for better light and then do a full sweep of the area. Once it was clearer they searched the area but found nothing to raise any suspicion, the ground just looked like it had been kicked as if someone had fallen over or a dog had tried to dig a hole but no grave and certainly no body, if only they known just how close they had actually been to Sam's grave.

Scarlett caught the update on the news, and was relieved, even if it had been a lucky escape, she knew she had planted the evidence she needed to and was pretty sure there was no evidence of her left on Sam's body, but she knew she would never be able to be completely certain, so she just had to hope that his body would never be found!

The thought of Sam's body being found had been enough to scare Richard into leaving just as she wanted him to, so at least she didn't need to waste any more time or energy, worrying about him. Now she just had to convince her mum and Chloe that Sam had left town and wasn't coming back any time soon.

Chapter Fourteen

Scarlett decided that if it looked like Sam's card had been used, then people would think he was still alive, but as lots of cash machines and shops had CCTV she knew she couldn't just go to her local shop and buy something on his card, it needed to be somewhere further away, someone not connected to Sam and ideally somewhere with no cameras, so she decided to just start driving and see where she ended up, and in the back of her mind she was also thinking about what to do when she got to where she was going, and wondered if she could find a homeless person and maybe convince them to take the card from her.

She started looking in doorways and bus shelters to see if she could spot anyone who might be able to help. She didn't have to wait long, she had probably been driving for about 30mins and saw a man sleeping in a bus shelter, and with a quick glance round, she couldn't see any cameras, but she still parked a bit further down the road, to make sure she stayed un-detected. She pulled her hood up and put her sunglasses on, as a way of trying to disguise herself a little bit and walked up to the man in the bus shelter who looked like he was sleeping, she knelt down and told him she needed his help, and she had money for him, he didn't say anything he just sat up and listened, Scarlett took Sam's credit card out of her pocket along with his mobile phone, she used her sleeve pulled down over her hand so she didn't leave any prints on either of them, she put them both on the floor next to the man. She had written the pin number on the back and she told him, to take the credit card and treat himself, it was her treat but the deal was that he had do what she asked, which was that he would send a text message she had already typed into the phone, at some time later that day and then destroy the sim card and the phone, and he had to promise that he would never tell ANYONE, he looked at her and nodded, a bit dazed and confused as to what was happening and then she walked off quickly and headed back to her car.

She knew that this poor homeless man would not hesitate to take her up on her offer, there were so many things he needed to keep himself safe and warm and he could now go and get it all. The message she had typed out would hopefully convince Marie and Chloe that Sam had left and wasn't missing, it said "I'm ok, please don't worry about me, I just need some space and time on my own, I don't want to hurt anyone but I'm feeling extremely overwhelmed by everything at the moment and just need a break, please give me the space and time I need, don't try and contact me, I will come home when I'm ready, I'm sorry, Sam xxx" that would throw them off for a little while, she hoped although she knew they would find his message difficult to accept without trying to find out more, this was going to take time.

For a split second she felt a pang of guilt as this was all part of her big plan starting to come to fruition, she did love Sam, of course she did, he was her brother after all and if she hadn't had him growing up, who knows what would have happened to her, he had been a good brother to her but now he was the obstacle stopping her from getting what she wanted and she had to sacrifice him. She had felt so much pain when she lost her dad, and she never wanted to feel that sort of pain again, so she needed to make sure she got this right, this was all for Chloe.

Scarlett was thinking, that what happened with Richard and Sam the other night worked in her favor but she still needed to act like she didn't know what was really going on, and she needed people to think Sam had gone, or that Richard might be involved somehow, she decided the next thing she needed to do was ring her mum and try to convince her that Sam had upped and left and she hadn't been able to stop him, but it was all lies.

"What's the matter Scarlett, I'm at work, I really shouldn't be answering my phone unless it's an emergency" she sounded pretty annoyed, Scarlett thought to herself

"Well, I think it might be an emergency mum, I can't find Sam, he is not at work, he is not answering his phone either, and there are clothes missing from his wardrobe, I think he has left"

"What do you mean, left? I heard him leave the house this morning, so he can't have gone too far, he might just be busy and that's why he's not answering his phone, it's not like you to get so worried, what's going on?"

"Did you see his face yesterday?"

"Yes I did, but he said he didn't want to talk about it, so I didn't push him"

"Well maybe you should have, because Richard hit him! and Sam thinks he hurt Chloe as well, so this morning after you left he was getting really angry saying he was going to sort this out once and for all, he was planning to go round to Richards and have it out with him, I told him he couldn't just go storming round there accusing him of hurting his own daughter, but Sam was so angry he wouldn't listen, and before I could do anything to stop him, he had grabbed a load of stuff from his room and stormed out of the house, I tried to follow him but I couldn't find him, I've been trying to call him and he isn't answering and Richard isn't answering his phone either" she thought to herself, how good a liar she was starting to become.

"Oh what a stupid boy, what is he thinking getting on the wrong side of Richard? I understand he wants to protect Chloe and find out what happened but if he really believes that Richard had anything to do with breaking her arm what does he think he would do to him? What makes him think

166

Richard is responsible anyway, just because he wasn't happy about them moving away, he is a single dad trying to protect his daughter, so who wouldn't have been a bit shocked at the news, I'm sure he is just worried about her, we should not jump to conclusions, we all know he has a temper and clearly Sam saw that the other night but that does not mean he would ever hurt his own daughter does it! I will try ringing Sam myself and see if he answers the phone to me"

Scarlett reminded her mum that people did think Richard had something to do with Elizabeth's death but Marie quickly dismissed that idea saying at the time it was just stupid busy bodies sticking their noses where they were not wanted and they had no idea what was really going on. Scarlett could tell she felt protective of Richard, especially having now read her diary and she wondered what she would be feeling right now.

"Richard did not have anything to do with that Scarlett" it still hurt to think that anyone would think that about him "we just need to find Sam and stop him doing anything stupid"

Marie could not get hold of Sam after trying to ring him several times, so she left him a voice message hoping he would pick it up before going to Richards, but she was starting to get a little bit worried so she managed to get out of work early and headed straight home. She waited till she had pulled up and parked on the drive and tried Sam again, she closed her eyes and took a deep breath, praying that he was ok and almost preparing herself for entering the house, what would await her? She did not need this right now, why would Sam be so reckless it was not like him at all to behave like this, this was the sort of behavior she would expect from Scarlett but not her precious Sam, if was back home then she would be having a serious conversation with him about all this.

"I do hope he is okay, I really don't want him getting into fights with Richard, if only he knew he was his dad, I'm not sure how Richard will react if he goes over there and starts kicking off" she planned to quickly get changed and then head out and try to find Sam, she ran up the stairs got changed, but before she went back downstairs she checked Sam's room, Scarlett was right, it was a mess and there were things missing, she felt quite concerned now and ran straight back down and was heading to the door when suddenly she noticed her lovely rug in the living room was missing but with more important things to think about right at that moment, she pushed the thought to the back of her head and rushed out the door, jumped back in her car and headed out again desperately looking for Sam. She had managed to get hold of Scarlett who said she was looking for Sam, too but she was really at Pixie's house, who was completely unaware of what was going on.

She drove round almost every street searching for Sam, whilst also ringing anyone she could think of to see if anyone had seen him. She decided she needed to go to the one place she hoped he hadn't gone, Chloe and Richards house.

She soon she found herself parked up outside their house, there was no car on the drive and no lights on in the house, she got out of her car and walked up to the front door, knocking loudly and waiting for Richard to come and answer if he was there but he didn't, which was very frustrating and also added to her fear and panic, if Sam wasn't here, the last place she could think of looking, then where on earth could he be, and why wasn't he answering his phone?

She decided to just go and check round the back and see if she could see through any of the windows, she had to be sure no one was here before she left, because she didn't know what to do or where to go after this. When she got round to the back of the house, she could see through the kitchen window, she pushed her face up to the glass to get a proper look but all she could see was a mess, empty food wrappers and beer bottles all over the place, he had obviously had a bad couple of days with Chloe in the hospital and the stress of all the falling out that had happened. She knocked on the back door but as expected, Richard didn't answer, so with a heavy heart she walked back round to the front of the house and got back into her car, trying to think if there was anywhere else that Sam might have gone, but she couldn't think of anywhere.

She wanted to ring the police because now she was starting to get really worried and she was almost certain that something must have happened and that he was quite likely in trouble somehow, but she knew it had not yet been 24 hours so the police would not really be that interested and would probably just tell her to go home and wait for him to turn up or contact her, he was a grown man after all, so less than 24hrs without contact they would probably have told her that happens all the time, but it didn't with Sam, this was not normal at all.

Frustratingly she knew the only thing she could do right now was just that, to stay at home and wait, because if she tried to carry on looking for him, where would she go? She had tired everywhere and everyone she could think of, she just hoped that he had changed his mind and decided to be on his own somewhere quiet for a while to gather his thoughts and clear his head and then he would just come home when he was ready, she knew more than anyone else how overwhelming life could be sometimes

The only other place Marie thought Sam might possibly have gone, was the hospital to see Chloe since she had been kept in overnight, she didn't drive there to check as she knew Scarlett had phoned there earlier but maybe he hadn't been there before, so was now was on his way and it was just bad luck that neither her or Scarlett had found him along the way. She was now mainly just praying for a phone call, just to hear his voice and know that he was ok, she needed to know he was ok, why wouldn't he just call her back? Or if he couldn't call her back, why? What on earth was going on?

Scarlett had to be very careful how she behaved from now on, along with what she said and how she said it, it was going to be extremely difficult, but she could not let anyone become suspicious of what had really happened or what she had done. She would have to play dumb and say that she hadn't spoken to Sam or seen Sam and she needed to act as normal as possible around her mum, but it wasn't like her mum was likely to notice anyway, so she probably wouldn't have to act very different at all around her.

Marie had not been home long, before Scarlett got back, she had barely walked through the door when Marie started…

"Where is he? what if something bad has happened to him?" Her voice cracked at the thought of what she had just said, she knew her relationship with Scarlett was strained but she was the only one she had right now and she was scared, so she needed Scarlett more now, than ever before

"I have not seen or spoken to him, why don't we sit down and have a cup of tea, I think we need to gather our thoughts, and come up with a plan" Scarlett was gritting her teeth as she didn't want to sit down and drink tea with her mum, but she had to look like she was worried about Sam too and in this situation, most people would come together to support each other, so that's what she needed to do with her mum.

"I think we need to ring the police" Marie said quite sternly, this was not the time for tea, she wanted to find her son

"There is no point ringing the police, it has not been 24 hours yet, they will just tell you they are not able to help! Scarlett quickly added, that was the last thing she wanted her mum to do, she needed to hold her off for as long as possible, she knew the police would be involved eventually but she was not quite ready. She wanted more time to get herself prepared.

"I know it has not been 24 hours yet, but if we explain the situation then they may take it more seriously, and might be able to help us somehow now, I may not be able to file an official missing person's report but they must be able to give us some advice, I cannot just sit here till it has reached 24 hours, I will go mad, and I certainly will not be able to sleep! At the very least, they might be able to trace Sam's phone, or check local CCTV, or maybe they could try and get in touch with Richard if we tell them what happened the other night"

"I could go to the hospital, Scarlett said "I think Chloe is still there, I know I rang earlier and she said she had not seen him but I could go back and see if anything has changed, lets hold off ringing the police for now, just until we know for certain that we can't find him, we don't want to waste the police's time do we"

"Ok, yes you could do that, good idea, you can see if Chloe has seen or heard from Sam or even her dad since you last spoke, I did wonder on my way back actually that maybe that's where he could be heading possibly, so you might see him, hopefully that is where he decided to head instead of going to see Richard but if he is not there, then I am not waiting any longer, I will be ringing the police as I really don't know where else he could be, I don't know where else to try and look for him and we have never gone this long without speaking to each other in person or on the phone" this highly annoyed Scarlett, as that just wasn't the same for her and Marie.

It was early evening now and was getting dark, Scarlett and Marie had spent most of the afternoon either looking for Sam, calling friends or trying to call him time and time again, It felt stupid to Scarlett to be out looking for her brother when she knew he was dead so she wouldn't find him or be bringing him home but no one else knew that of course so she had to act like she didn't know that and go along with it, everything felt a bit like a dream, was this really happening just how she had imagined it, her mum certainly seemed to be worried.

She went to see Chloe, who just as Scarlett knew already, hadn't seen or heard from Sam since she rang him to tell her what had happened to her arm and the possible concussion, and she had not seen her dad since he dropped her off at the hospital that morning, she was going to be sent home tomorrow and still couldn't get hold of Richard or Sam after trying to ring them several times and she was starting to get worried, surely one of them would want to know she was ok and when she would be able to come home, which one of them would be coming to pick her up? she told Chloe that Sam didn't believe her broken arm was an accident and seemed very angry, she hoped he and her dad had not got into another fight, that was the last thing she wanted or needed when she was trying to convince her dad to be ok with her and Sam's plans to move away with each other.

Scarlett rang Marie and told her what Chloe had said to her, she tried to convince her once more not to ring the police yet but Marie was not going to wait any longer, she knew something was not right. By the time Scarlett got home Marie had spoken to the police, she had been told exactly what she expected annoyingly, and that was to stay at home and keep trying to call Sam, but to ring back once it had been 24 hours, so that is what they had both done, stayed home waiting and waiting and waiting, it was going to be a very long night if he didn't turn up, which Scarlett knew of course that he wouldn't. Marie was so worried, and she planned to stay up ALL night if she had to, where on earth was he, he wouldn't have just left, she knew it deep in her heart as his mum, that he would never just leave like that, on his own and without saying goodbye to anyone, something was definitely wrong.

Chapter Fifteen

The next morning just as the sun was rising and starting to stream in through the window Marie woke with a jolt, she had clearly fallen asleep while sitting on the sofa, and hadn't even shut the curtains. She was on her own so Scarlett must have gone upstairs to bed, she hoped that Sam had come home while she had been asleep so ran upstairs to check but as she opened his bedroom door, it was just as it had been the day before, there was no sign of him, she sat down on his bed and began to cry she felt so helpless and just wanted to know he was ok.

Scarlett woke up to the sound of her mum crying and wondered just for a moment, what she would be thinking if it was Scarlett that was missing? She probably wouldn't care she thought to herself. She felt exhausted, yesterday had taken more of a toll on her than she first realised, she didn't go in to see if her mum was ok, she didn't care, she waited for her to stop crying and head downstairs before she got up, she knew going downstairs and being with Marie was going to be more awkward than normal.

Marie made her way downstairs and walked into the kitchen and filled the kettle up, just like any other morning, almost without thinking about what she was doing, she reached into the cupboard and took out 3 mugs without really thinking that Sam wasn't there, it was instinct to get 3 mugs out, she realised what she had done but left the mug out, she still hoped he would just walk through the door any minute now and she glanced at the front door, willing it to open but nothing happened.

Scarlett was making her way downstairs and went into the living room to turn on the tv, having the news on would be better than nothing as the silence in the house was unbearable, and she didn't know what to say to her mum, so she thought there needed to be some background noise, nothing they needed to pay attention to, they had enough on their minds already, she spotted that Marie had got 3 mugs out but decided not to say anything.

Just as Marie was waiting for the kettle to boil, she was standing there, in a bit of a trance not really paying attention to what she was doing, but then she heard the news, "possible body found in wooded area in Peterborough" she span round so she could give the news her full attention, her eyes never left the screen as she listened intently to the rest of the news bulletin terrified that it might be Sam.

Scarlett couldn't believe it, this couldn't be happening, what if they had found Sam's body, she wasn't feeling quite so confident anymore, and started to question in her head, what if she hadn't done something right or forgotten to do something, she was panicking massively as she continued to listen to the news, praying that they didn't say anything else

The news reader continued "A man was out walking his dog in the early hours of this morning, and suspects that he has uncovered a make shift grave in Holme Wood, police are asking people to avoid the area at this time while they are investigating and they cannot give us any further details at this stage"

Marie just looked at Scarlett and started to say, "you don't think…." but then burst into tears, "oh god, what if that's Sam" she tried to say through her tears.

Scarlett knew there was nothing she could do now, other than to just try and keep her mum calm "Mum, you can't think like that, if it was Sam then the police would have called us wouldn't they, and they don't even know if it is a body they have found and also why would Sam be in Holme woods anyway? It is not somewhere he normally goes is it, try not to panic mum"

"Well, I am not waiting around, Marie said angrily, I am ringing them again now, I have waited long enough I want to know where my son is, RIGHT NOW! You need to try and stay calm mum, and also be rational about this, but she ignored her and stormed out of the room

Scarlett started pacing the room, she had not really thought about IF Sam's body was ever found, although she had planted evidence to frame Richard she had not really thought about exactly how that would play out, and she was now feeling extremely nervous, they can't have found him, surely she thought to herself, I really hope not. The next thing she heard, was Marie on the phone, obviously talking to the police

"Yes I know it has not yet been a full 24 hours, but considering what has just been on the news, and what I told you yesterday about my son, and his girlfriend's father, and the close proximity to where we live are you seriously going to tell me that there is not the slightest chance that my son could be dead and in that grave" she held back her tears "I don't want it to be my son, of course

I don't, but he has not come home and he is still not answering his phone and no one has seen him, or heard from him, this is NOT normal for Sam so PLEASE listen to me when I say so something must have happened to him, I am his mother, we are extremely close and I know something is wrong, please help me"

Scarlett, had never heard her mum sound so angry and upset in the same breath

"No, please don't put me on hold, I want someone to take my details, and find my son!"

The police officer on the other end of the line, had put her through to someone more senior who had reassured her that they were taking her call seriously, and they would need certain details from her and then they could create a file for Sam, so she gave them all the information that she could, and hung up. She went back into the living room and explained everything to Scarlett

"So what happens now?" Scarlett asked

"I'm not really sure if I'm honest, but fingers crossed they find him, and more importantly that he turns out to be ok!"

"At least they are taking it seriously now, but let's keep praying as well, just in case" Scarlett was quite proud of that, it sounded like she actually cared just for a moment.

"I'm not ready to give up hope, I will never give up hope, not unless I see his dead body, he is out there somewhere, I know he is, he has not just vanished into thin air has he" we just need to find him, and if the police won't help then I'll hire a private detective"

"You do know how expensive private detectives are don't you mum, where are you going to get the money from?

"I don't care Scarlett, this is my son we are talking about and I will do whatever it takes to find him"

Scarlett thought to herself that even now, Marie was still showing that Sam was her favorite, more than ever she still couldn't bring herself to talk to her like she was her daughter, it was like Marie only had 1 child, her perfect Sam. Marie started to feel a bit unsteady on her feet. She was exhausted, so she decided she was going to try and have a nap, as she was about to go upstairs she noticed again that her rug was missing, it struck her as odd, now she was thinking about it, because it was always there, it had never moved since the day she brought it, so where was it, and why had someone moved it? she asked Scarlett if she knew.

Scarlett noticed her mum looking at where the rug usually was, and had to think of a story quickly as she couldn't exactly tell her she had wrapped Sam's body in it and buried him with it could she!

"I spilt some wine on it the other night, so I took it to get dry cleaned as I couldn't get the stain out, and I've just not had chance to get it back yet, sorry. I would say how is it you have only just noticed, but you obviously have more important things on your mind right now"

"Oh ok" she said, slightly suspicious "I could have sworn it was still there this morning but obviously not, I can't think straight at the minute, I'm going upstairs to have lie down"

"Good idea, if anything happens I will come and tell you"

She wished her mum had not spotted the rug as now she would have to try and replace it, she could not pretend it was being cleaned forever. Just then, her phone pinged, it was the message she had told the homeless man to send to her, her mum and Chloe, she felt relieved that he had done what she had asked him, she could show her mum once she woke up and wondered if Chloe would message her about it.

Chapter Sixteen

Richard had driven off, and made his way up the road, he looked in his rear view mirror and saw Scarlett shutting the door behind him, if she thought this was over she had better think again, as this was far from over, she was not going to banish him from his home and his daughter, he was so angry, he would never hit a woman but in that moment he had seriously wanted to hurt Scarlett, how had she become such a vindictive, evil monster?

He couldn't believe that her childhood had really been as bad as she said, was Marie really like Scarlett had described? He didn't want to believe it, as that wasn't the Marie he knew, or use to

189

know, maybe Scarlett just wanted people to feel sorry for her?.

His head was all over the place, and he just didn't know what to do next, but what he did know was that he needed to go somewhere, anywhere to get away from Scarlett, he thought it was probably best to head away from Peterborough, and try to find somewhere he could stop and then try to collect his thoughts. He decided to head for the motorway and planned to drive for a little while and then stop at service station with a hotel when he saw one.

He spotted one not long after he had started driving, so he turned off the motorway and decided to stop and see if he could check into the hotel, at least that way he would have somewhere to stay the night if he didn't leave before then.

Success, he managed to book a room and found himself standing outside the room ready to unlock the door and let himself in, he didn't know exactly how long he would be here but he knew it wouldn't be long, he couldn't let Scarlett win, he needed to stop her and soon.

He sat on the edge of the bed and let out a big sigh, he felt drained but he wasn't ready to give in, he went and had a shower to wake himself up a bit, he then made himself a cup of tea and once he found some paper and a pen, he planned to write down everything that had happened and everything he could remember Scarlett saying to him/telling him while it was still fresh in his mind, he knew It would be her word against his, but if he could remember some of the things she said it might help him, he had to try anything at this point, because if this all went wrong he would find himself in prison for a murder he didn't commit and he would lose Chloe for good, he couldn't even bear to let himself think what that would be like, he loved her so much, he had only ever wanted to protect her and he couldn't do that if he ended up in prison.

He really didn't want to leave Chloe behind, or just walk away from his home and friends but he also couldn't take any risks at this stage, as he didn't know that Scarlett wouldn't do what she said she would do, he was not going down for Sam's murder, she was!

He just had to work out what to do next, but where on earth did he begin? This wasn't something any normal person had to deal with usually in their life. As he drank his tea and let the hot liquid warm up his insides and help him relax slightly he couldn't help shaking his head in utter disbelief that this was happening.

He decided that he had no other choice, he needed to call his brother John, but he knew it would be a bit awkward as they hadn't spoken for quite a while and John was now married to one of Richards old flames, Alexa, who he also hadn't seen or spoken to for quite a long time but he didn't know what else to do, he felt that this was his only hope.

His brother lived in Northumberland and when Elizabeth had died, he had tried to convince Richard to bring Chloe and move there so they could all be closer together and John could be there to support them through that difficult time, but Richard just could not bear to leave the house that he had lived in for so long with Elizabeth and he also didn't want to up root Chloe and take her away from everything she knew, even if she had only been 6 at the time he didn't want to risk Chloe resenting him as she got older for leaving their family home or her mums grave behind and setting up a new life, even though Northumberland was a beautiful part of the country, and in all honesty he had wanted/needed his brothers support at the time, but he just couldn't admit it, but now he was seriously wishing they had gone as he would have been able to keep Chloe away from Scarlett.

He knew this time he couldn't deal with all this on his own and so he dialled his brothers number anxiously waiting for someone to answer, he just hoped someone was there to pick up

It was John that answered the phone who was very surprised that it was Richard on the other end, but he was happy as they had missed each other a lot, even if neither of them would say it out loud to each other.

It felt like old times, there were no cross words or animosity between them, Richard decided for now, not to tell them anything about what was going on, but he did ask if he could go and stay with them for a few days, John had said that of course that was ok and asked when would he like to come, he was a bit taken a back when Richard said Now, but they agreed the best thing to do was for Richard to get some sleep first and then try and leave in the early hours so he could beat the traffic.

Richard couldn't sleep so it was pointless really, all he kept doing was playing the day's events through his mind, thinking about Chloe and Elizabeth, and how he betrayed them with Marie, he must have nodded off though as he was suddenly woken up when his alarm starting beeping at 4am.

He got himself together, made sure he had everything and checked out, then he was back in his car and on the road again.

Several hours later he was pulling onto John and Alexa's driveway, suddenly feeling very nervous about everything he needed to tell them, he just hoped they believed him and didn't think he had gone mad.

After all the usual pleasantries, Richard was in their living room with them both looking at him, they could tell something was wrong, so they asked him what was going on, but how could he just come out and say it?

He really didn't know where to start, this was not something normal he was about to tell them and once he told them, he knew he would be dragging them into this mess too, so he felt guilty but also knew that he couldn't keep this to himself.

"Urm.... Do you remember the Fords, who use to live a couple of doors down from us?"

"Yes of course" John replied "Scarlett is best friends with Chloe isn't she, and isn't Chloe going out with Sam the last time I heard?"

"Yes, well.... It has all gone horribly wrong and I really do mean HORRIBLY WRONG" he put his head in his hands.

"What's happened?" Alexa asked, concerned

"You won't believe what I'm about to tell you, but Scarlett admitted to me that she has killed her brother, Sam" he waited to see how they would react.

"WHAT?" they both said at the same time, they were both completely shocked.

"Yep, and that's not the worst of it all, she claims she has planted evidence on his body, that would frame me for his murder, if he is ever found"

For what felt like a lifetime they all sat in silence just looking at each other, he was scared they didn't believe what he was telling them, why would they it did sound crazy, he couldn't bare the silence any longer.

"Please say something" he said

"Why the hell would she do that? what's wrong with her, you don't believe her do you? Surely this is just some sick joke? John was struggling to take in what Richard had just told him not because he didn't think his brother was telling him the truth but because this was just unbelievable that if this was true, Scarlett had killed her brother!

"You didn't see her John, it was like a switch had been flipped in her head and she just turned into a complete psycho, it was like she was actually enjoying it and she didn't even seem to care at all about what she had done to her own brother, she even showed me a picture of his body, this was supposed to be someone she loved dearly, so yes I do believe her, enough to do what she said anyway, she basically told me to disappear, she wants me to leave town and never come back, leave Chloe and cut all ties with everyone I know and love, and never try to contact anyone, otherwise she says she will tip off the police, I just don't know what to do"

"Oh Richard, I'm so sorry" John said

"Me too" Alexa said "We need to come up with a plan, she can't be allowed to get away with this"

"Apparently she wants Chloe all to herself, I'm not sure if she has some weird crush on her or what, but I need to make sure Chloe is safe, and I need her to know that I have not just upped and left her on her own and I need to warn her about Scarlett, but without Scarlett finding out"

"Could you try phoning her?" Alexa asked

"I don't think I can take the chance, in case Scarlett is with her – she told me she has planted my DNA on Sam's body and stupidly we had a fight a few nights ago and I hit him in the face, so it doesn't look good does it"

"Ok then, let's try and come up with a few things we could try, we can then work out pros and cons for each and go from there, we need to keep you out of the picture for now, and maintain Chloe's safety as much as we can" John responded

"I think we need someone that neither of them know to try and maybe go and see Chloe, Alexa would you help?"

"Sure, but do you think that's safe, how will I get in touch with Chloe, I can't just turn up on the doorstop can I?! I need to make sure I'm safe as well as Chloe" she said, sounding quite worried, if everything they had just been told was true, none of them really knew just how dangerous Scarlett might be

"I understand your concern Alexa and sadly I can't promise it will be 100% safe, but maybe John could go with you, but stay out of sight? Then you're not on your own if something was to happen, and to get in touch, maybe you could just send her quick and innocent message about being in the area and wanting to pop in, do you think that could work?" he needed reassurance, because of course he didn't know if Alexa would be safe, or if Chloe was safe or if any of this would even work, and he was terrified, but they couldn't give up, they had to try something and no one could come up with an alternative solution.

"Ok then, let's work out what to send to Chloe and we can get that message sent" John said, putting his hand on Richards shoulder, to try and offer some reassurance, he really hoped he could help his brother get out of this mess, but was also worried about his wife and niece.

The next morning, Alexa had sent a text message to Chloe saying she was a friend of her uncle Johns, she didn't want to reveal exactly who she was in case Scarlett found out, because if Scarlett knew her true connection to John, then she was likely to work out that they were in contact with Richard, and thankfully, not many people knew that she and Richard had ever been together.

She explained to Chloe that she was going to be in the area in a day or 2 and asked if she could possibly pop in and say hello as she had heard a lot about Chloe and seen lots of family photos too so thought it would be nice to meet her in person, this also meant she would know it was Chloe when she got there, not Scarlett.

Chloe had seemed a bit unsure to start with, she had so much going on and really didn't need this as well, but Alexa reassured her she wouldn't outstay her welcome so she had agreed, it would be nice to hear how her uncle was doing, as she hadn't seen him so long and really missed him, maybe with everything that was going on, she could reach out to him for support.

Chapter Seventeen

Sam was dead, and Scarlett was the only one that knew, that made her feel quite powerful knowing she was the only one, there was a sense of achievement, knowing the pain she was causing for her mum, she was finally in control and she loved it!

The message hadn't really worked as neither Marie or Chloe believed that Sam would ever leave and say goodbye in a text, so they were adamant now that something was very wrong so everyone else started to believe the same thing and the longer he was missing, the more concerned everyone was starting to get, and Scarlett had to remember to play along, even though she could see how upset her mum was, which pleased her a great deal, her mum had never cared when Scarlett was upset about anything so she deserved this, but she hated seeing Chloe in so much pain, she didn't like the fact that it was her actions that was causing this pain and upset for Chloe but she knew it would all be for the greater good eventually and that Chloe would understand that one day, but she would need to give her time to heal first, she couldn't rush her.

Sam's body would hopefully never be found, and she was pretty sure that if after 7 years there was no sign of life when someone is thought to be missing that families would officially be able to declare them dead.

Unfortunately her plan to throw everyone off by giving Sam's bank card and phone to that homeless man, didn't work as he got caught on CCTV, but when he was picked up by the police, thankfully he hadn't dropped her in it, he had just told them he found the card on the floor and as he had been caught using the card in a shop, but with wireless payments he hadn't needed to know the pin, so it meant he didn't have to tell them how he knew it or if he did know it, and because he had destroyed the phone just like Scarlett had told him, he didn't need to explain that either, but once the Police knew about the card, they seemed to become suspicious and started to wonder if the message from Sam's phone could be fake as well as they couldn't trace his phone, and there had been no sightings of him, they now believed that something had happened to him and that this could be part of the killers plot to throw them off. Thankfully Scarlett had wiped down the phone, before she gave it to the homeless man, and he had smashed it up and thrown it in the river just as she told him to, so hopefully no one would ever find it or be able to link it in any way back to her but she needed to be more careful as that little stunt had almost back fired, she could have got herself in a lot of trouble.

Blackmailing Richard meant he was out of the picture too, he had not even tried to fight it, he had been extremely angry but didn't think twice about packing up and going, leaving Chloe behind – showed just how selfish he really was, it had been such a thrill for scarlett when she told him exactly what she had done and how she had planted evidence to frame him if he ever came back, ever told anyone or ever tried to make contact with Chloe, it would just be 1 quick call to the police to tip them off about where Sam's body was. Her plan had worked perfectly, Sam was out of their lives forever and Marie and Richard were being punished for all their lies and what they did to Elizabeth and Matthew.

Chloe could be with her properly now, 100%, no more sneaking around having an affair, they could be a proper couple, Chloe had no one else now and she would need comforting, but she would assume that Scarlett was distraught at the loss of her brother and would comfort her too, so already being lovers they would only grow closer once Chloe realised Sam was never coming back. Scarlett didn't want to upset Chloe, she would never want to do anything to upset or hurt her but this had been the only way she could make sure that she got what she wanted as well as punish her mum at the same time. If they hadn't done what they had, and her dad was still here, then none of this would have happened as she knew she wouldn't haven't turned out to be so vengeful, this was all their fault! why had she not killed her mum instead, or even Richard rather than Sam? simply because she wanted them to suffer as much as possible and she wanted them to both see the damage they had caused.

It had been a very long week and everyone was still worried and upset about where Sam might be or what might have happened to him, now Richard had disappeared too, Chloe didn't want to stay at home on her own, so Scarlett told her she could stay with her and Marie for as long as she needed to, and that together they would try and figure out what to do next, but while everyone thought Sam was still missing Chloe was in limbo and a little confused by her feelings, not knowing what to do next, so Scarlett needed to make sure she didn't push things too quickly, as she knew that Chloe wouldn't be too keen right now to carry on having an affair as she was so worried about Sam, she was so close now though, so she wanted to make sure she was by her side offering her as much support as she could and hopefully proving to Chloe that Scarlett was the only person she really needed in her life now and that she would know that Scarlett would never leave her side.

As Chloe walked into their house, she told Scarlett that it was unbearable not knowing where he was or if he was ok, and she was also worried about her dad, Scarlett felt guilty for causing Chloe so much pain but she knew it would be worth it in the end. Chloe said that she couldn't bear to sleep alone in Sam's bed knowing he wasn't there, so she ended up sharing with Scarlett, in Scarlett's room after all they had been through it didn't feel awkward and Chloe just wanted to be held till she fell asleep, she knew that they needed to look after each other now more than ever and be a comfort to each other too. She was so tired and emotionally drained, she didn't want to sleep, she wanted to be out there looking for Sam, but she knew she needed to rest and as she lay her head down she realised how heavy her body felt and soon closed her eyes and started to drift off to sleep, she felt safe with Scarlett so she allowed herself to relax fully and fall asleep.

Scarlett was tired too, she lay next to Chloe and felt the tension of the last few weeks disappear from her body. Her eye lids felt extremely heavy as she lay next to Chloe, with her arms around her, but as watched her sleeping, she gently stroked her hair and breathed in her scent, her heart was full, a smile crept across her face, she finally had everything she had always wanted and she whispered "It's all ok now Chloe I promise, you are safe with me. Sam is gone, your dad is gone and we can finally be together properly, it has always been you Chloe, for as long as I can remember and I just wish we could have been together as a real couple sooner, rather than having to keep it a secret from everyone. Sam was always in the way, so I was forced to take matters into my own hands and that's why I killed Sam and I have framed your dad, nothing is in our way now Chloe, nothing at all and the people that have done us wrong have been punished once and for all, I love you so much" she kissed Chloe on her forehead before her eyes finally closed.

Chloe suddenly opened her eyes WIDE, she hadn't been fully asleep and so she had heard EVERYTHING that Scarlett had just said, her heart was beating so fast she could hear the blood pumping in her ears, she felt hot and realised she was breathing heavily, she looked out the corner of her eye to check if scarlett was really asleep, she needed to get out of there and quickly, she slowly slid out the side of bed, she was already dressed luckily, so only needed to grab her shoes and bag which both were downstairs.

She crept down the stairs, all the time listening out for any sound from Scarlett, she had stayed at their house so many times that she was now thankful she knew exactly where all the creaky steps were and made sure she avoided them. She felt like she couldn't breathe and soon realised she was holding her breath, she didn't want to make any noise in case she woke Scarlett up, she could feel the tears began to prick her eyes, she felt scared, confused and upset and she just needed to get out of there as quickly as she could.

As she shut the door gently behind her, she took a deep breath in, letting the cold night air fill her lungs, she took one last look back at the house and up at Scarlett's bedroom window and then started to run, she ran faster than she had ever run before and thankfully she knew exactly where she needed to go and exactly who she needed to tell, she couldn't wat to get there.

She stopped just before she got to where she was heading and had one final check behind her to make sure no one was following her, she was so paranoid that Scarlett had woken up and seen her leave the house, but there was no one behind her, it was late at night and the streets were empty, most people would be in bed she thought rationally and then carried on running to her final destination, she couldn't wait to reach a safe place and she was now only 5 minutes away.

Chapter Eighteen

Chloe had finally reached Frank and Grace Bailey's house and started hammering on their door, she was so scared that Scarlett was following her and she needed them to open the door as fast as they could so that she could get inside, and be safe.

Whilst continuously looking over her shoulder, as soon as Frank started to open the door, Chloe pushed her way in, slammed it shut behind them making sure all the locks were done up and then fell on the floor in a heap, with tears pouring down her cheeks uncontrollably, she just couldn't hold them in any longer, she pulled her legs to her and held them tightly and buried her head in them she knew Frank would wonder what was going on but she just wanted to be invisible.

Frank bent down to put his arm around her, he was extremely concerned, this wasn't like Chloe "What on earth has happened?" he asked as he tried to look at her and check she wasn't hurt

Trying to talk through her tears she managed to tell him what had just happened, and word for word what scarlett had said to her. As the words came out, she felt herself relax just a little bit, It didn't make her feel any better but it felt like such a relief to have someone she could tell all this to, Frank was like a dad to her and she knew she would be ok with him, but she just could not stop the tears from falling.

Frank's wife Grace had been asleep upstairs but the noise had woken her up and so she came down to see what was going on. Chloe felt guilty for having woken her up, as soon as Grace saw the state Chloe was in, she knew something was wrong, so as Frank stood up to explain, she went straight to her and sat with her, putting her arms around her in replace of Frank, she was like a second mum and a big hug was just what she needed right there in that moment. Chloe whispered to her that she was sorry and Grace told her not to worry about it and gave her a kiss on her forehead "Come on love, let's get you off this cold floor" she said, whilst helping Chloe get up and into the living room so that she could sit on the sofa.

Chloe couldn't help looking back at the front door "you're safe here sweetie, the doors are all locked and we have an alarm" Grace reassured her, she could see how frightened she was.

Frank followed them in and tried to ask Chloe a few questions but he didn't want to upset her any further so he was trying to tread carefully "Did you do anything, or say anything to Scarlett before you left? take your time"

"No" she said as she tried to wipe her tears "I just had to get out of there as fast as I could, and I ran straight to you, I didn't know where else to go. I don't understand what is happening, why didn't I realise any of this sooner, I knew she was starting to act a bit strangely but I just thought she felt left out because I was dating Sam. Oh god" It was like she was just realising something and she stopped herself saying anything else

Frank could tell that she was holding something back or had maybe just remembered something "Is there something you're not telling us Chloe?" he asked gently

For a minute she had forgotten that he was a Police officer, but she knew she would not be able to get away with lying to him, she looked at Grace for reassurance and she responded by saying "you know you can always trust us Chloe, we want to help you, but we can't do that if you don't tell us everything"

She didn't know how else to tell them, so she just came out and said it how it was "Me and Scarlett were…. more…. than friends" she waited, nervously for their reaction but neither of them seemed shocked or surprised and frank just said "When you say more than friends, what are we talking about exactly?"

Grace looked over at him as if to say, don't be so stupid, you know what she means, and he must

have been able to sense her looking at him, as he then said "Sorry Chloe, I appreciate that's a rather personal question but I do have to get all the facts right, I don't want to get something wrong and mess any of this up"

"It's ok Frank, I do understand, I'm just a bit embarrassed that's all, no one else knew about us and now this is happening"

"It's ok, just take a deep breath, and when you're ready just tell me"

"We were having an affair, behind Sam's back, I feel so guilty, how did I let myself get sucked in by her, what have I done" her heart felt so broken and it hurt more than ever before, apart from when her mum passed away, the tears came faster and stronger.

"It is NOT your fault Chloe, if you loved each other, there was a bond between you, why would you ever suspect that something was wrong? and why would you EVER think that something like this would happen? Is there any chance she could be lying or she had a nightmare and was talking in her sleep?

"I don't know, I don't think so, she seemed very calm, not like she had had a nightmare or anything and if she is lying why would you say something like that? it's not really something you would make up is it, and it's not like she had been drinking or anything like that either, so why else would she say it unless it was true, plus she said it when she thought I was asleep, I think that's the ONLY reason she said it, she wouldn't exactly want anyone to know this would she, I wouldn't have thought!

Her chest suddenly felt really tight, she felt like she was starting to have a panic attack, Grace tried to help her calm down and Frank went to go and get her a drink from the kitchen, as she started to gain her breath back, Grace got a blanket, and wrapped it round her, then she just sat there with her, holding her in her arms, and when she started to cry again, she just made sure she was there for her, she was safe here and they would look after her like she was their own.

Grace felt Chloe's shoulders drop and her body starting to relax and knew they needed to get this right, she knew that Frank would feel like he now had the weight of the world on his shoulders as he would not want to let Chloe down. They just had to hope and pray that if Sam wasn't ok that at least Richard might be, otherwise they were not sure just how this poor girl would ever recover.

"I think we all need to try and get some sleep" Grace said as she stood up

"Yes" Frank agreed "that's all we can do for now and then tomorrow we can talk it all through

properly, when our heads are a bit clearer and we have had some rest, Scarlett isn't going anywhere for now so we have a bit of time" but as he looked at Chloe she had laid her head down and falling asleep, he grabbed another blanket off the arm of the sofa and gently laid it over her, he didn't want her to get cold in the night and he was grateful that for now she was able to sleep, it gave her just a slight respite from her pain. Grace and Frank headed upstairs to bed, and he knew they had a tough time ahead of them, poor Chloe, he really hoped they could protect her this time, as he felt like he had failed her when she lost her mum, even though at the time he had suspicions something wasn't right, he didn't do anything, but this time he would not let anything slip past him, he would do right by Chloe no matter what and he knew he had Grace by his side as support.

Chapter Nineteen

Frank and Grace had been together since they were 18, they had met at a disco where Frank was DJ'ing and as Grace recalls, she knew the moment she saw him that she wanted Frank to be her boyfriend and by the time they were 21 they were married.

Chloe always thought when she saw their wedding photos that they both looked like movie stars as Grace was so beautiful in her wedding dress and Frank looked so handsome and dapper in his wedding suit, with his long hair, which always made her smile.

Grace had always wanted children one day but was in no rush as she still felt so young, and she wanted to make the most of her life before settling down and becoming a mum, Frank was already a young police cadet by the time they got married and he wasn't interested in starting a family at their age, so they decided it was something for the future, but as they approached their 30's both with great careers in teaching and the police force, they still weren't sure about starting a family but decided to give things a try, sadly though it soon became apparent that it wasn't to be for them, but they had both come round to the idea and found that they couldn't bear the thought of having an empty house forever, so they decided that they wanted to start fostering and threw themselves into the community making it a better place to live for everyone, they would organise events, hold drop in meetings for people to reach out if they were in need and they very quickly became the beating heart of the village.

Everyone knew Frank and Grace and everyone loved them too. Many of the troubled youngsters made it through the doors of the Bailey household and all had their lives transformed for the better, they were amazing. As their fostering started to take off they even made the decision to move to a bigger house so that they could foster even more children, they thrived on being able to help people, as well as being able to help people to see that they can also help themselves sometimes.

Chloe and her dad had certainly needed them a lot when Elizabeth died and Chloe would sometimes stay the night with Grace and Frank so she could be with other children rather than alone in her bedroom with just her thoughts, and it would give her dad a bit of a break as well.

Scarlett had been the same when Matthew died and she would sometimes go with Chloe and stay for tea with the Baileys or play in their garden with all the other children when it was summer. The atmosphere was so much better than in their own houses as everyone was so sad all the time and even though they were small they felt guilty for feeling happy sometimes or wanting to laugh and do something fun, at the Baileys none of that mattered, they could just be normal little girls playing with their friends, not the 2 little girls that had lost a parent and who everyone looked at differently just felt sorry for all the time.

They were allowed to make the bedrooms their own so some of the children would draw on the wall or write a message for the other children to see, Grace and Frank felt that it was important the children felt like this was home, and that they had something that was theirs, obviously there were rules too and you were always expected at the dinner table on time and to be clean and presentable but most of the time they just wanted the children to have fun and be happy as lots of them had troubled pasts or had experienced a horrible upbringing - they just needed love in their lives and it really did made everything better for them.

They had both kept in touch with Frank and Grace for quite a while and then one day Scarlett just stopped, said she didn't need them anymore, the Baileys said that was ok but to always remember where they were if she ever needed them again. For Chloe they felt like family to her so she never stopped going to see them like she would anyone else in her family and Frank had been helping her to start thinking about her future as she was considering a career in the police force like him.

Chloe couldn't help thinking now, how it was such a shame that whatever Scarlett had been going through all this time, that she couldn't have reached out to Frank and Grace, after everything they had done for her, they had helped her so much when she was growing up, and they would have helped her again, and maybe all of this could have been prevented, but she knew it was too late for that now.

Chapter Twenty

The next morning, Chloe was woken by the smell of bacon, she felt safe at Frank and Graces house, and although she knew she wouldn't be able to hide here forever there was no way she was ready to see Scarlett yet, she couldn't even stand the thought of seeing her, let alone actually doing it and being in the same room as her, she could hardly bring herself to even say her name. She went to get herself up from the sofa and felt a bit light headed, so she slowly made her way to the door, resting again the door frame to steady herself, she took a deep breath and then made her way to the kitchen, she didn't know what Franks plans were yet and she didn't know how she could ever be in the same room as Scarlett again, she didn't even know if she could stomach the lovely breakfast Frank was cooking, she had never felt pain like it, apart from when her mum passed away, her eyes were red and stinging from all the crying, it was unbearable and she could understand now, that if you were in that much pain, how easy it might be to feel you wanted to end it all and make the pain stop! that's how her mum must have felt she thought to herself.

As she walked into the kitchen she could see through the patio doors that Grace was outside feeding the bird and in the kitchen she could see Frank busy preparing breakfast, he hadn't noticed her yet so she just stood there watching him for a while, Frank and Grace were like parents to Chloe even though by age they were more like grandparents, Chloe didn't have any of her grandparents as they had all sadly passed away now. Sometimes she wished that Frank was her dad, or that her own dad could be more like Frank, this is how she imagined life would have been if her mum was still here, coming down at the weekend to the smell of a fry up, and seeing her mum pottering about in the kitchen, she missed her so much and really wished more than anything that she was here now, wrapping her arms around her and telling her everything was going to be ok, while Chloe breathed in the scent of her perfume and felt the gentle kiss on her head, like she use to when she was little.

Frank turned round and spotted her "Is everything ok?" he asked

"Yes sorry, I didn't mean to creep up on you, I was just admiring your cooking skills"

He smiled and chuckled "Thank You, I love cooking but it's not quite the same now it's just me and Grace, I miss not having a house full of kids to cook for anymore, so I thought since you were our guest that I would treat you to my special full English breakfast, take a seat food is nearly ready"

Frank and Grace sadly didn't see many of the children they fostered anymore, as they had all grown up and had all now moved out, most of them would still come and visit but not as often now they were all older, and some even had their own families now. She could sense that Frank and Grace missed having a busy house and people to look after and there was a sadness about them at times, not that ever tried to show it - they were both very strong people who you could always rely on and they had been close friends to Chloe's family for as long as she could remember which was a comfort to her.

As Chloe went to sit down she saw that the dining table was covered in paperwork, she asked Frank what it all was whilst trying not to look at it in case any of it was personal, she didn't want to disturb anything.

"Oh, I got up early and started making some notes, I didn't want to forget anything you told me last night as we need to make sure we get this right, you can just put it all in a pile for now if that's ok, and I can sort it all out later"

Chloe started to pile it all together, just as Grace came back into the house, she was SO grateful that she had them both to help her with this, they had always been there to look out for her and now felt no different, she knew they would never let her down.

"Thank you" she said as she turned and smiled as she put the pages to one side

"For what?" they both asked

"All of this, taking me in last night, listening to my rants and putting up with all the tears and now helping me to figure it all out"

"That's what we are here for, and we always will be, we couldn't save your mum but we will not let anything happen to you Chloe, I promise you! do we know where your dad is yet?" Frank asked

"No, I've tried calling him again but he is still not answering and now his mailbox is full"

"Ok, we will park that for now then, but I think we will have to try and track him down at some point as it does feel a little suspicious that he seems to have gone missing at the exact same time as Sam, so we need to make sure he is ok, because if Scarlett told you the truth about getting rid of him too, what did she mean?

"I'm scared, what if Scarlett has done something to him too? I can't lose Sam and my dad, I really don't think I can face seeing Scarlett again Frank, please tell me I don't have to"

"I know, how worried you must be Chloe, we all are but please try not to worry for now, I know that's easier said than done, but until we hear anything different we have to assume that he's safe, ok! and as for Scarlett, I'm afraid it will look very suspicious if you just suddenly stop answering her calls or going to see her won't it, because that is not normal at all in your friendship or relationship from what you have told me"

"I know, but just the thought of being anywhere near her makes me feel physically sick, what am I supposed to do, or say to her? this is so hard, I don't think I can do this, I don't want to do this, this is such a horrible situation to be in, I hate it"

Grace put her arm round Chloe's shoulders "You can do this Chloe, we believe in you because you are going to do what you need to do, for Sam! You need to know what really happened to him to be able to deal with your grief and we need to catch a killer who is currently still out there living her life, acting like everything is normal because we need to keep you safe as well, just because she says she loves you and you can now be together, if what she has said is true then we have to assume she is capable of anything and you did have a dream to work for the police one day didn't you? I know it's not the situation you wished you were in, but it could be good practice, as if you can handle this, you would probably be able to handle anything"

"I know you're right, you're always right, I just need a little bit of time, maybe I could text her for now, try and convince her everything is ok, I could say that I got up early and wanted to go home, I didn't want to disturb her so I crept out, and yes I do still have that dream or I did anyway, I'm not sure after all of this, that is what I want any more though"

She paused for a moment and looked out over the garden through the window, she could see the birds scrambling for the last of the food Grace had put out for them, it looked so peaceful out there, inside she felt anything but peaceful or blissful, she stood there watching the birds, happy eating their food, and totally unaware of all this mess, she wished she could swap places with them, she just couldn't believe what was happening - how had her life gone so horribly wrong, one minute she had a boyfriend who she was moving away to start a family with, she had a best friend and lover who she couldn't bear to be a part from but now was a 25 year old, who had lost her mum, lost Sam, her dad appeared to have disappeared too, and when she needed her best friend more than ever, she didn't have her either because she was the reason Sam was dead and she would NEVER forgive her for that but she knew she would do EVERYTHING she could to make sure she was locked away for a VERY long time, she wasn't going to get away with this!!

She suddenly realised her fists were clenched really tight and there were tears falling down her cheeks, she felt so angry

"Are you ok Chloe?" Grace looked concerned

"I'm just so angry, why did she do this to me, to Sam, to her mum? What makes someone kill their own brother, she's a psychopath"

"Like you said, she loves you, people will do anything for love and sometimes that means hurting people that get in their way, if she wanted more and felt Sam or your dad was stopping her she obviously felt she needed to act fast"

Frank said "If you still want to join the police force one day, you will start to learn that sadly there are a lot of crazy and dangerous people in this world"

Chloe held her head in her hands, she had a headache, and was so tired, this is just a nightmare, she thought to herself, an absolute nightmare, would she ever be cut out for the police force?

"Come and sit down, try and eat something if you can and make sure you have a drink too, then we can start to work this out together, and figure out exactly what to do next"

Chapter Twenty One

Scarlett wasn't sure what was going on but she had started to notice that Chloe was behaving a bit strange recently, She didn't seem to want to spend much time with her at the minute and also wanted to stay at her own house again, which both confused and annoyed Scarlett as Chloe had originally said she couldn't bear to stay in the house on her own and they had been so close, she had loved having Chloe at her house and in her bed so they could fall asleep in each other's arms every night.

Was she being a bit irrational? Chloe was allowed to stay in her own house if that's what she wanted to do, and Scarlett didn't want her to feel overwhelmed or push her into anything before she was ready and she had to try not to appear too clingy in case that put Chloe off, but it did feel like she was starting to be a bit distant with her, was she having seconds thoughts about them being together?

Scarlett was worried, but she did have to remind herself that Chloe still thought Sam was missing, and that meant that for Chloe, there was still hope that he might come back and so she wasn't just going to suddenly forget about him and move on with Scarlett, she was planning to move away with him, after all.

Chloe might not have verbally acknowledged exactly how she was feeling but Scarlett imagined it was probably similar to her mum although not quite as bad as for her, things had just not been the same at all since Sam had disappeared she was a shadow of former self, she was so withdrawn, tired, upset, anxious and just completely worn down, she wasn't sleeping properly and most days was getting sent home from work early as she just wasn't coping, Scarlett was really quite enjoying it as this was all part of her punishment that she wanted for her mum but if Chloe was feeling even half of any of those feelings then she really did need to give her the time and space she needed, for now at least but this couldn't go on forever they would have to accept Sam was gone and never coming back one day and she would be there to pick up the pieces for Chloe, she didn't care what happened to her mum.

For Chloe, she was never going to share with Scarlett exactly how she felt, at least not until this was all over and she was in prison, how could she, because her feelings had changed now and if she told Scarlett she was worried Sam was dead rather than having hope that one day he might come back which although she was extremely worried about him, that is how she had felt until Scarlett's confession so surely she would start to be a bit suspicious, but to be honest although she knew she couldn't completely ignore her, she couldn't be anywhere near her, and just the thought of the things they had done together knowing now, what she has done, made her feel physically sick.

She couldn't help wondering what she had done wrong, why was all this happening to her? first her mum, now her boyfriend and Scarlett might not have killed him, but she was also prepared to take her dad away from her too, why was there so much hatred? Why did she want to cause so much pain for her? and she wouldn't even have her best friend to help her through all this either, it hurt so much and she just wanted it to all be wrong, she didn't want to believe that Sam was dead or that her best friend was the one to kill him, how would she ever get over this, right now she didn't know, but what she did know was that after everything she had heard and now seen at Scarlets house, she didn't for one second think that any of this wasn't true, she hated her so much, more than she thought she could ever hate anyone and that just spurred her on more to make sure that she did all that she could to help the police catch her and punish her for what she had done, she couldn't be allowed to get away with this, no way in hell, that just was not an option, at all.

Chapter Twenty Two

Frank had given Chloe some good advice about what to do next, and she did now felt slightly more prepared for seeing Scarlett, although not quite yet. She should have been at work but she rang in to say she still needed some more time, they understood as they knew Sam was still missing, and had already told her to take all the time she needed, they could manage without her. She had been ready to go back, she needed to go back to work but not after this, she needed to know where Sam was and what really happened the day he went missing, and she just couldn't face being around other people right now, trying to put on a brave face or making polite conversation with people and pretending everything was ok, not now she knew there was a real possibility that Sam might be dead, she didn't want to believe it.

Grace had told her she could stay as long as she wanted or needed to but Frank had reminded her that she would need to try and act as normal as possible when she was around Scarlett again so that she did not suspect anything. Chloe knew this was going to be one of the hardest things she had ever had to do, apart from burying her mum at just 6 years old and she still couldn't quite believe that Scarlett would cause her this much pain, knowing what she had been through losing her mum, she knew exactly what it felt like to miss someone and she wished she could bring her dad back every day so why would she inflict that pain on Chloe and Marie again?

Chloe was worried what Scarlett would do when she woke up and saw she wasn't there, but she didn't have to wait long as she noticed she had a voicemail from her waiting on her phone, thankfully it didn't sound like she suspected anything or was angry, she was simply asking why she had left so early and without saying goodbye to her.

Chloe knew she would have to reply but could not stand the thought of hearing her voice, not after last night so she decided to send her a quick text in response, hoping that would buy her a bit of time, her stomach churned just seeing her name and sending her a message, she had to try and come across as normal as possible.

"Sorry I didn't get to see you before I left, I woke up super early and just couldn't get back to sleep, I didn't want to disturb you so I decided to creep out and I walked home, I had a shower and got myself some breakfast, but then ended up falling sleep on the sofa. I think I just need a few hours alone if that's ok, being at yours is just so hard while Sam is still missing, but I promise I will call you later xx" a tear fell down her cheek

She felt so disgusted pretending to be so nice to her and acting like they were still best friends and lovers, she was annoyed with herself, how had she let herself get involved that way? she was absolutely dreading the moment she would have to come face to face with her again, how could she possibly not let on how she was really feeling, surely her face would give it away, frank had given her some tips to try and deal with that and also kept reminding her why she was doing this but it still felt like a really a big ask of her, to go into Scarlett's room and basically snoop for evidence, then try to get a photo of anything and all whilst making sure she didn't disturb anything because she could NOT under any circumstances let Scarlett suspect a thing, what was she even looking for anyway, this was not normal, this was not Chloe, she wasn't someone who creeped around peoples house and snooped through someone's personal belongings but she needed answers and if this was the only way then she just had to do it, however uncomfortable it felt, this was for Sam, and possibly her dad as she still couldn't get hold of him. She thought of Marie, what had become of her precious son and daughter, where had it all gone wrong, she couldn't help wondering if Marie knew anything, and if she did would she protect Scarlett no matter what, or would she be like Chloe and be prepared to do anything for Sam and get Scarlett locked up?

She couldn't exactly just come out and ask her directly but maybe she could have a quick chat with her the next time she saw her, just to see how she would react or see if she said anything that was out of sorts, but she did also need to remember that this was a mother extremely upset that her son was missing and she didn't want to upset her any further, this made her think of her dad again, where the hell was he? she really hope he was ok, as Scarlett did mention getting him out of the picture, what did that mean exactly? She didn't know if he even knew about Sam because they both seemed to go missing at the same time, neither of them were answering their phones and no one had seen either of them since that morning either, something didn't feel right especially after everything Scarlett had said, she was really worried now.

There is no way he can be involved is there, surely not? she thought, but instantly felt guilty for letting herself think that, he might not be perfect and he certainly had a temper after all she had seen the fight he had with Sam, only a few days ago but he wouldn't kill anyone, he couldn't and she truly believed that, although it hadn't always been that way.

She could still remember the speculation that everyone thought he was involved in her mums death and how everyone use to look at him or cross the road to avoid him, and there had been a moment where she did find herself questioning everything but she knew that her dad was not capable of anything like that, he loved them very much and those first 6 years together as a family had been perfect in Chloe's mind, I think his guilt came from not being able to save my mum or being able to protect me from finding her and all the pain that followed. There was never any evidence at all that it was anything other than suicide, that mum carried out completely on her own, and so eventually people started to forgive and forgot.

Chloe would also always fight his corner if anyone said anything bad about her dad but it had been quite tough for a long time and she couldn't go through all that again, but she was worried that people might start to question her dad again if he didn't come home soon, she realised she was crying again her heart felt so heavy, right now she had no idea at all how she would ever be ok again, how on earth would all this mess sort itself out, and where would they all end up at the end of this, she just didn't know.

She would need to make sure no one was in the house when she went to have a look in Scarlett's bedroom, she was so nervous about doing this but if Scarlett really had killed Sam then she needed to find the evidence to prove it.

She picked a day when she knew both Scarlett and Marie would be at work, she still had a key so she could let herself in, and people in the street had seen her there plenty of times so she wouldn't raise any suspicions going to the house even if no one else was there. She unlocked the door and found herself standing in the hallway, scared to take another step, dread filled her whole body as she didn't know what she might found and she felt extremely sick too. She really didn't want to do this, but she knew she had no choice.

As she reached Scarlett's room at the top of the stairs, she realised that the last time she had been there was the night Scarlett told her what she did, it was only a couple of days ago but it still felt very uncomfortable and she couldn't help reliving that moment as she stood there preparing herself for opening her wardrobe, she glanced at the picture of the 2 of them together stuck to the top of her mirror, and a tear fell, Chloe couldn't believe this was happening, she wanted to go to sleep, and wake up to realise this was all just a very bad dream, but she knew it wasn't, she opened the wardrobe slowly, and once open she almost fell backwards when she saw what was inside, it was like a shrine to Chloe, SO many pictures, things from days out they had shared like cinema tickets and bus tickets, even a lock of what looked like her hair, when the hell did she get that? Chloe thought to herself, it was really creepy and she spotted the picture of Sam and Marie, both with their eyes scratched out, with "I HATE YOU" written across her mums face and You NEED to Die written across Sam's.

She couldn't believe it, how had she not seen any of this before? How had she not realised how Scarlett really felt about her mum or Sam? This felt so disturbing and dark she wanted to run out of there and back to the safety of the Bailey's but she knew she needed to take some pictures with her phone, she thought she had a diary, Chloe was sure she had seen something under her pillow once, she went to check and there it was, but it was locked, she quickly looked around trying to find a key but she couldn't see anything obvious that would fit, so she took a picture of that as well as that's all she could, and she didn't want to disturb anything.

She couldn't find Scarlett's laptop, and doubted she needed it for work but maybe she had taken it with her, surely what she had just seen in her wardrobe would be enough, she hoped she had done all that she could, she didn't want to let Frank or Grace down but she needed to get out of there, it was like the air was thicker and she felt like she couldn't breathe properly.

As she went to go, she bumped into the end of bed and it moved slightly, she panicked as she knew she need to leave everything exactly how it was, but as she looked down, she saw what looked like a tiny drop of blood near the foot of the bed, Chloe couldn't be sure that's what it was but it definitely looked like blood to her, she took a picture and put the bed back, before heading out the house as fast she could, making sure to look as normal and calm as possible as she left the front door and was back on the street, she didn't want any of the neighbours thinking she was acting suspiciously.

She headed back to Frank and Grace's House. Frank was at work by the time she got back, so Grace told her to head to the station as Frank would be waiting for her.

At the station Frank told Chloe she had done really well, they had enough to get a warrant now. He told her, that he would say it was an anonymous tip off for now, as he wanted to keep Chloe's name out of it for as long as he could, but he did warn her that he might not be able to do that forever. Chloe felt numb as she knew this was only just the beginning and she was also worried that this still didn't prove if Sam was actually dead or not, and if he was, where his body was, so she didn't feel like she had any answers, just more questions, Frank must have been able to sense that she was worried as he told her not to worry, and explained that this was the way in, that they needed and not to give up hope, there would be more to come after the search and Scarlett's questioning.

Chloe wondered what else they would find, they were bound to get her diary unlocked, she wasn't prepared for what they might find as she knew there would be things about her in there and once they found the creepy shrine as well, they were bound to want to know more from Chloe about her involvement with Scarlett, it was going to be so embarrassing, but she did hope that there would be something about Sam or her dad in there, not that she would want to read it, but it might explain a few things and give her the answers she do desperately needed.

Chapter Twenty Three

A couple of days later, Chloe was back at home waiting for Alexa to arrive. Alexa soon found herself outside Chloe and Richard's house, she checked behind her before knocking on the door and she could just about see John lurking behind a bush just a little way down the road, this was a big risk and she just hoped they could pull it off.

She kept the visit short, but she learnt a lot in a short space of time, it turned out, that Chloe had not been given Richard's letter, and Scarlett had not mentioned anything about seeing him, or him going away, so Chloe had been extremely worried about her dad. Chloe also knew all about what

Scarlett had done to Sam, as Scarlett had said it in her sleep.

Chloe had told Alexa to keep her dad hidden for as long as possible, and wait till she got in touch again to say it was safe to come home. She would need to fill frank in on all of this but told Alexa she wouldn't keep her updated along the way, just in case Scarlett become suspicious of her texting someone all the time, which Alexa agreed was probable the safest idea. Everyone was really scared of Scarlett so they all needed to be extremely careful.

Alexa and John headed back home and planned to fill Richard in on all that they knew, they wished they could do more to help or keep Chloe safe, but they also knew why they needed to keep their distance, and Frank and Grace seemed to be doing a good job of looking out for her.

Richard would have to continue hiding in Northumberland until he knew it was safe for him to return home, but at least now Chloe knew that he was safe and hadn't just run away and left her on her own, and she had been able to fill Frank in with everything she knew about what happened to her dad, so hopefully this would help the case against Scarlett

They all really hoped this would get sorted out soon, for everyone's sake as it was just so awful what was happening, but at the same time they still couldn't quite believe this was all actually happening, it was a nightmare.

———

When Chloe had filled Frank in, he couldn't believe it, he was shocked at the lengths Scarlett was prepared to go in order to cover her own tracks and get rid of anyone she saw as being in her way. He believed she was a very dangerous person and they needed to arrest her as soon as possible, he prepped Chloe about what would be happening next and talked to her about what was best for her to do in terms of where she stayed, what she did and what she said to Scarlett in order to keep herself safe, and she was also going to have to try and help make sure Scarlett was where the police wanted her to be and at the right time as they were going to raid her house.

They now had enough suspicion to get a warrant and they needed to see what evidence they could find in the house, based on Chloe's findings which they couldn't use in court, they needed to find it for themselves but it put them in a good position and hopefully everything was still going to be there and when they went through every inch of her car, her room and the house they might even find more, there was always a slight level of excitement for Frank when he caught criminals and had enough to arrest them but this time it felt different, he wished this wasn't happening, what had happened to Scarlett, he had known her since she was little, like Chloe and never thought that one day he would be arresting her, and certainly not for murder of her own brother, this case felt more sad than exciting.

Chapter Twenty Four

Scarlett was somewhere where she never, ever thought she would end up, she was in prison, how had it all gone so terribly wrong? This was never a part of her plan and she was VERY angry that this was yet another thing keeping her from Chloe, but she had convinced herself that it would all be ok, because Chloe would wait for her, and if she wrote to her every week, and if Chloe came and visited, then she knew she could get through this.

She knew her mum would never want to come and see her, and to be honest she didn't care, she hated Marie and everything she had done, if Sam had never been born then none of this would have happened in her mind, Marie had not even be able to look at her in court when she was sentenced, Scarlet had finally broken her, and she still had the upper hand as no one knew where Sam was buried so Marie couldn't even have a proper funeral. Richard had been in court too as once the police had all the evidence to lock her up, they knew it was safe for him to come back to Peterborough and be with Chloe again, and he needed to be in court so that he could look her directly in the eyes and let her know she had lost.

She knew being in prison also meant she couldn't go and see her Grandad, and that really hurt, she knew he was so old and poorly now, she was worried that he might pass away before she would be released and that really did upset her, she wondered if maybe she could ask Chloe to go and see him in her place, if she did the heart thing on his hand like she would normally do then he would think she was still there with him and he wouldn't know that any of this was going on.

Pixie and Josh had also been in court that day and Scarlett felt sad to see how much she had upset them both, especially Pixie because she hadn't had chance to explain any of this to her, she hadn't been able to end things properly and they had been in a relationship which Scarlett thought if Chloe had not existed could have worked, she really liked Pixie but had never really considered her in all of this, or Josh who had been a big help to her in helping her conceal her sexuality, she had been so determined to get what she wanted that she forgot that they were both likely to get hurt in the process and she couldn't even say sorry now.

Neither Pixie or Josh really knew what to do, they just couldn't believe that someone they knew and loved had turned out to be a killer and so they felt they had no choice but to go and see her in court and see and hear everything for themselves, and they were so shocked at some of the things that came out, they were also very aware of their emotions in front of everyone else as no one knew about Pixie, so to everyone else she was just the bar manager where Scarlett worked so yes she might be shocked or upset but felt that she couldn't really show just how much because that might have seemed a bit weird, not that anyone was really paying anyone other than Scarlett or Chloe any attention at all as that day had been about them!

As for Josh, everyone thought he was the boyfriend that didn't really exist so he needed to show a bit more emotion, but he was supposed to be a straight man so was trying very hard to not go over the top, but to be honest, he had been so close to Scarlett that in some ways it did feel like they had been in a relationship, so all his emotions were very real. They both knew this nightmare, wasn't going to end for a while as people would be talking about this for months even years in the pub where they both worked, which they both hated the thought of, they were never going to be able to get away from it.

It was so unfair, all this pain and suffering caused by just one young lady supposedly in love and with one major vendetta towards her mum, brother and Richard it was horrible to watch in court as she had been sentenced as everyone felt relief but it didn't take away any of the pain that they were all feeling.

As for Scarlet she still truly believed that she and Chloe were soul mates and that they loved each other more than anyone else, Richard might have been back in the picture again, but that was not going to stop her being with Chloe whether he liked it or not, although she knew there would be A LOT of resistance from him after everything that had happened but she genuinely believed it was all going to work out because she believed that Chloe would never leave her all alone in prison, and that she would stand by her and wait for her to get out.

No matter what had happened, Chloe now knew for certain, just what Scarlett had done and Scarlett knew that Chloe had played a part in getting her arrested as she had been there when the police turned up at her house with a warrant and when they found enough to arrest her, stupidly she wanted to try and run, not that she would have got far as there were police everywhere, but Chloe convinced her to hand herself in and reassured her it would all be ok, owning up and confessing would help her, but to start with she tried to deny it all, she knew they didn't have Sam's body and she just made sure she didn't say anything that might incriminate herself but whilst they were interviewing her, the evidence was starting to stack up, they had found so much when they searched her home, that there was no way she was getting out of this easily and she decided she couldn't stay quiet any longer. She needed to try and explain what had happened and make them realise why she did it, she genuinely thought this would help her get a lighter sentence, she was so naïve.

There were photos, voice recordings, drawings and then her diary, along with the knife she used to stab Sam, for some reason she just hadn't been able to dispose of the thing that she had used to take her brother's life and stupidly she had basically kept a record of absolutely everything, assuming it was all private and no one would ever find any of it. They even found blood and hair samples that matched Sam's in the boot of her car from where she had put him in the boot to dispose of his body, and there had also been a snagged thread from the rug that her mum told the police had been taken to the cleaners the day Sam went missing, but had never come back.

How could she have been so stupid, the evidence was stacking up, there was SO much they could use against her, but she knew that the knife, the voice recorder and her diary had been hidden under the floorboards, which were under her bed so how had they found them? But then she remembered all those crime dramas she liked to watch, and in those, the police would literally turn houses upside down to make sure they didn't miss anything, they would empty drawers, turn beds upside down, nowhere was safe, so it was no wonder that they were able to find all the stuff, she thought she had hidden well.

She felt like such an idiot, her plan had been so meticulously thought out, how could she fail to plan hiding all the evidence better and she worried how Chloe would react, this was seriously make or break time now, as she had never even considered for second what would happen if she was caught.

This changed everything and she risked losing Chloe for good but she had surprised her by promising it would all be ok, she told her that she wasn't going to go anywhere, she would help Scarlett get through this no matter how long it took, so Scarlett didn't care about what had happened to her for now as her focus was still on being with Chloe, because that was all she had EVER wanted her whole entire life, and prison was just 1 more set back that she would need to deal with, in her mind it wasn't the end, but she was still extremely annoyed with herself that she was here, how had she been caught, and that temporarily she had been taken away from Chloe again, but she thought she had been really careful about what she did and said, and all the evidence was well hidden, so what was it that tipped the police off? But none of that mattered right now as the day Chloe was coming to visit was nearly here and Scarlett was so excited.

When the day finally arrived, she couldn't wait to see Chloe again, as the last time she had seen her was in court and she hadn't been able to speak to her let alone hug her or anything. As she walked in to the visiting room and headed to her table, she saw Chloe sat there waiting for her and her heart skipped a beat, she smiled and Chloe looked up and smiled back it felt so reassuring to scarlett but as she sat down, something didn't feel quite right and it felt like there was a bit of tension between them "maybe it's just because we are in a prison" she thought, Chloe might have felt a bit nervous being there, prisons are not normally somewhere most of us ever find ourselves, she tried to reach out and hold her hand but was quickly reminded by the guard that touching, was not allowed.

"I'm so glad you are here, I have been dying to see you" Scarlett said

"Ha, you've been dying to see me" Chloe scoffed "What like Sam? you have some nerve Scarlett, are you even sorry for what you have done? you have ruined my life do you actually understand that? I only came here today to tell you that this will be the last time you will EVER see or speak to me, as I want nothing else to do with you as long as I live"

Scarlett's mouth dropped open, she couldn't believe Chloe was saying these things to her, she was panicking a bit now and tried to think fast as to what she could say in return as she wanted to make sure she said the right thing, she didn't want to make things worse but how could she rectify this?

"I didn't mean to ruin your life Chloe, everything I did was for you, to protect you and give you a better life, with me, I thought we loved each other and I just needed to get rid of everyone that was in our way, they were no good for us Chloe, they didn't love us or look after us like they should have done, I was trying to save you from it all"

"That might have been YOUR family Scarlett, but it was not mine, and it certainly wasn't Sam's either. I don't love you Scarlett, not anymore, we were best friends, lovers and who knows where we would have ended up eventually, but that all ended the moment you decided to kill Sam and try to frame my Dad for killing him! Normal people don't do that! and you just don't get it do you, I HATE YOU, you have hurt me so much Scarlett, people that love each other don't do that to each other and it was me that helped get you caught, you were so blinded by what you were doing, you had no idea at all what was going on behind your back, you stupid idiot, why do you think I convinced you to hand yourself in, you needed to be locked up and punished for what you have done! not that it will bring Sam back, or ease my guilt of what we were doing behind his back, and I can't make any of that better now, because you have taken that chance away from me and you don't even seem to think you need to say sorry for anything"

"What do you mean, why are you saying these things, don't be like that Chloe, please I know you love me, you just might not want to admit it right now, you just need some time, and when I'm released we can be together again, I know it has all come as such a shock, but I understand why you convinced me to hand myself in, because it was the right thing to do, as much as I wanted to get away with it, running away would have been so much worse and you told me you loved me, that you would stay by my side and help me through this, why would you do all that if you never planned to stay by my side, why were you so determined to persuade me to hand myself in? surely you should have believed that I was innocent, certainly until it was proven otherwise, you clearly had no trust in me"

"You are not listening to me are you Scarlett? I helped the police, I was gathering evidence behind your back to help them catch you, you don't even realise where you went wrong do you? You confessed it to me, that first night I stayed at yours when we thought Sam was missing, you told me EVERYHTING while you thought I was sleeping, but I wasn't and I heard it ALL! I lied to you, to get you to hand yourself in, have you even got a conscious Scarlett? Don't you get it, having a conscious, having morals is part of our core, it's part of our very foundations as human beings and yours is contaminated now because of what you have done, you have spent months weaving a web full of deceit and lies and there is no fixing this, there is no way at all to un-do what you have done, this is the life you have chosen to create for yourself and its forever. Do you know, that it is actually quite a small percentage of killers that are women, we all have it in us to become criminals but most of us don't allow ourselves to travel that path, only the worst people give in to those dark urges, and that's YOU! I want nothing else to do with you, ever again, I'm so stupid to have ever loved you, I completely fell for it and look where we are now"

"You loved me and you don't now? That's a bit rich don't you think Chloe, if you had really loved Sam as much as you think, then you would never started having an affair with his sister would you, but you have enjoyed every minute you were with me, maybe it was a thrill for you to have us both so don't pretend you never thought what it might have been like if Sam was no longer in the picture but what do you expect from a girl that wasn't loved as a child, this is all my mums fault, not mine"

"A child who wasn't loved? You had everything Scarlett, a Mum who didn't kill herself and leave you all alone like mine did, a dad who doted on you, a brother who looked after you, made sure you were never on your own and loved you very much! what about me, you have had me by your side almost since the day we were born so how can you say you were not loved Scarlett and that still doesn't explain why you did what you did, what so you couldn't have me all to yourself so you decided to kill Sam? Do you know how sick and twisted that is, that the only option you thought you had was to murder your own brother just to be with me, even though we were already together, you need help, real help but not from me, we are done! You have tainted all our lives, you are like a stain on my favourite top that I can't get out no matter how much I try, so now need to throw away and forget about. I can't even look at you anymore, goodbye Scarlett"

"He was going to take you away from me Chloe, he had convinced you to abandon me and leave me all on my own, with my horrible mum or doesn't even like me, let alone love me, and so I had to stop him"

Chloe put her hand up to signal to the guard that she was ready to leave. How had she ever let herself fall in love with Scarlett, she was pure evil and she could see that now she just wished she had seen it sooner, and then maybe Sam would still be here, she didn't even seem sorry, she had never once said sorry for taking Sam away from Chloe, she simply saw him as an obstacle she needed to remove to get to her.

As Chloe walked away, she didn't once look back at Scarlett but could hear her shouting out to her clearly hoping for a reaction "You were related you know! Sam was your half-brother, my mum had an affair with your dad!" but Chloe just kept walking, rolling her eyes and sighing, more lies Scarlett she thought to herself, more stupid awful lies, she knew she was doing the right thing by walking out of her life for good

"You might not believe me but there is proof, my mum kept a diary how ironic she muttered under her breath as that's what had landed her in all this mess. Try asking your dad, did you never wonder why he was so against you being with Sam"

Chloe stopped and for a split second considered turning round one more time, to talk to Scarlett again but she just couldn't, she didn't believe that any of that could possibly be true, it was absurd and it was just a tactic to try and get her to stay, or maybe it was even a way to hurt her, maybe she wanted revenge on Chloe now.

Chloe was not going to indulge Scarlett's fantasies any longer and continued to walk away from her, when she was in hospital, she found out she was pregnant, so there was always going to be a little piece of Sam with her forever, she was going to make sure she lived her life to the best of her ability in honour of her mum and Sam, she was going to get her relationship back on track with her dad and was going to look into joining the police force with Frank and Graces help! She was not going to let Scarlett win, she would not be controlling her life anymore and she certainly would never see the baby and Chloe hoped that actually she would never even find out that he or she existed.

As the gates opened and she walked out of the prison, she sighed a big sigh of relief, prison was not a nice place to be at all and she was so glad she was out of there, knowing she would never go back. She spotted Richard, John, Alexa, Frank and Grace standing on the opposite side of the road, they all knew that meeting would have been very difficult for Chloe so wanted to be there to support her, as she walked over to them, she took a second to look up into the bright blue sky, the sun was beaming down on her and she smiled, it was like she was looking up at Sam and her mum, saying to them, that everything was going to be ok now, she always felt like she could feel their Prescence and although she was sad that they were no longer physically there with her, she was happy knowing they were both looking down on her, this was going to be the start of her brand new life and it excited her, she would not let any of them down, or her baby, who she couldn't wait to meet.

Scarlett was fuming that Chloe hadn't listened to her, and has just walked out! She knew it would come as a shock to her, but did she really not want to find out more? Why wouldn't she just believe her, Sam didn't either, Marie and Richard had fooled everyone for all this time and it wasn't fair. She hadn't even had the chance to ask Chloe about her Grandad, not that she thought she would help her now, not after this and as she saw the door close behind Chloe she broke down and started to cry, she couldn't do that while Chloe was still there, she didn't want her to see how upset she really was, this was NOT the plan, what would she do if Chloe never forgave her? That thought was just completely un-bearable for Scarlett to contemplate even for a second but she knew the reality was that she was going to be locked up for a long time, so how on earth would she be able to win Chloe back?

One thing was for sure, she was not going to give up, no matter what happened, she was going to win her back and get out of here so she could be back with her Grandad too, she just didn't know how yet.

THE END

Acknowledgements:

A Massive Thank You has to go to Lisa Johnson, Abigail Horne, Deanne Adams and Claire Clarke as without you, none of this would have been possible, you've all supported me, allowed me into your worlds and have taught me so much.

Thank You to my amazing friends (you know who you are) You are all very special to me, you are always there for me and I would be lost without you

A big thank you to my Daughter Maddi, my Parents Jenny and Terry, my Mother in law Jane and my Husband Nick for putting up with me whilst I've been writing the book, you have all supported right from the start and genuinely want me to succeed, I Love you all so much xxx

Thanks also has to go to my 2 Fur babies, Bailey and Pixie who are my indoor cats and have kept me company while I've spent hours in my office, writing the book

About the Author

Amy Braybrook lives with her Husband,
Daughter and 2 house cats in Peterborough.

To be a published author has been a dream of
Amy's since she was a very small child.

As well as publishing this book, she has also
published a short children's story that she wrote
for her daughter.

Amy loves to be creative and when she is not
writing, she is creating notebooks and other
books in her business Miss A.M.I

Thank You so much for buying and reading the book, it really means a lot to me and I hope you have enjoyed it.

If you would like to follow me, to see what else I do and hear about any future books please connect with me, using these links:

www.miss-ami.co.uk

www.facebook.com/MissAMIonline

www.instagram.com/miss_a.m.i_online

Printed in Great Britain
by Amazon

77566945R00163